Date: 4/5/11

JIMMY SNIFFLES VS The MUMMY

STONE ARCH BOOKS
www.stonearchbooks.com

Graphic Sparks are published by Stone Arch Books
151 Good Counsel Drive, P.O. Box 669
Mankato, Minnesota 56002
www.stonearchbooks.com

Library of Congress Cataloging-in-Publication Data
Nickel, Scott.
Jimmy Sniffles vs the Mummy / by Scott Nickel; illustrated by Steve Harpster.
p. cm. — (Graphic Sparks. Jimmy Sniffles)
ISBN 978-1-4342-1190-3 (library binding)
ISBN 978-1-4342-1390-7 (pbk.)
1. Graphic novels. [1. Graphic novels. 2. Mummies--Fiction.] I. Harpster, Steve, ill.
II. Title.
PZ7.7.N53Jim 2009

741.5'973—dc22   2008032061

Summary: Jimmy Sniffles and his class take a field trip to the museum. Some believe the
newest exhibit, the Mummy of Amun-Set, is cursed. At first, Jimmy doesn't believe the
frightful legend, but then some of the museum's artifacts go missing. Can the kid whose
nose knows track down the truth? Or will this mummy mystery finally stump his
super schnozz?

Creative Director: Heather Kindseth
Graphic Designer: Emily Harris

1 2 3 4 5 6 14 13 12 11 10 09

Printed in the United States of America

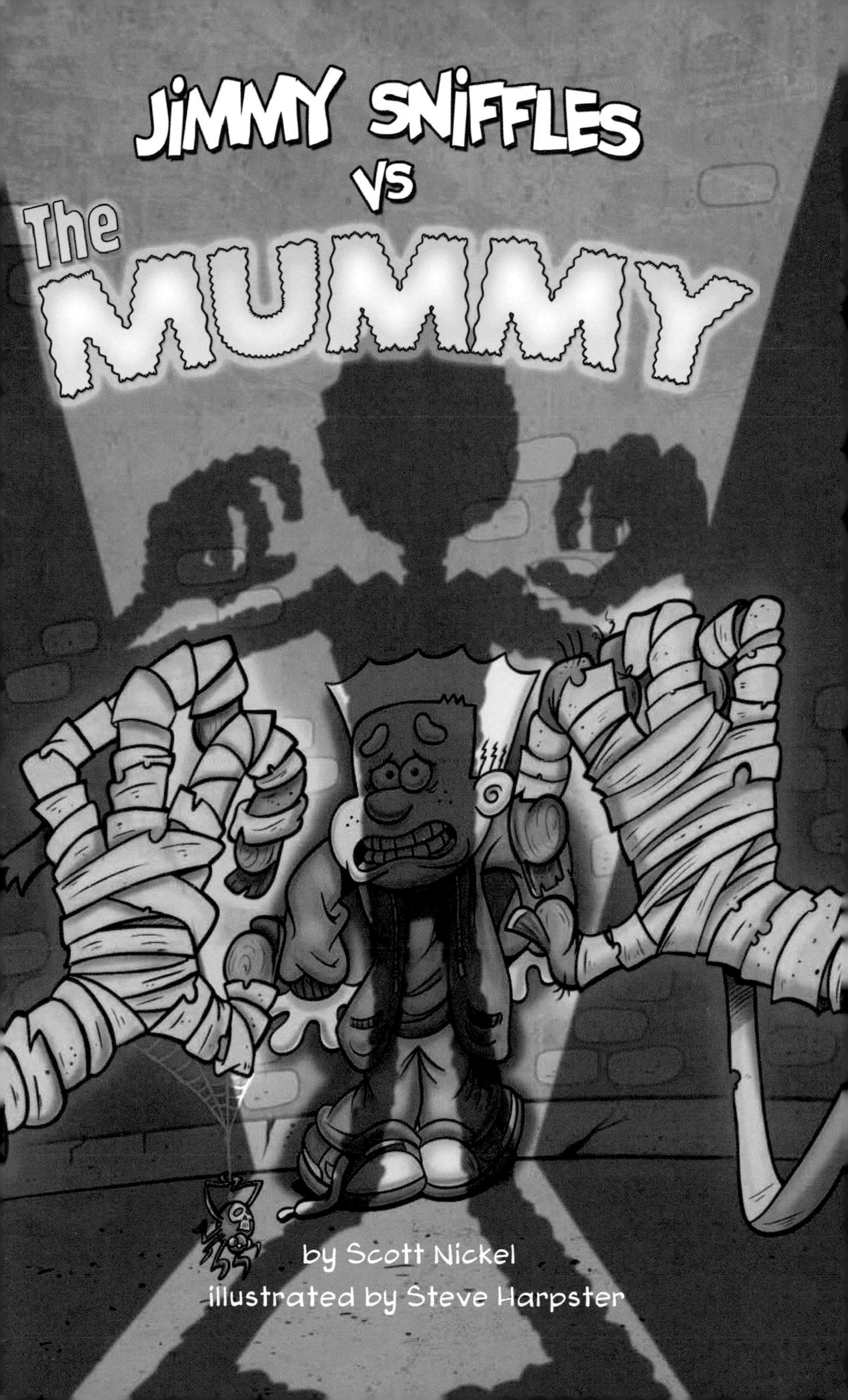
Jimmy Sniffles
vs
The Mummy
by Scott Nickel
illustrated by Steve Harpster

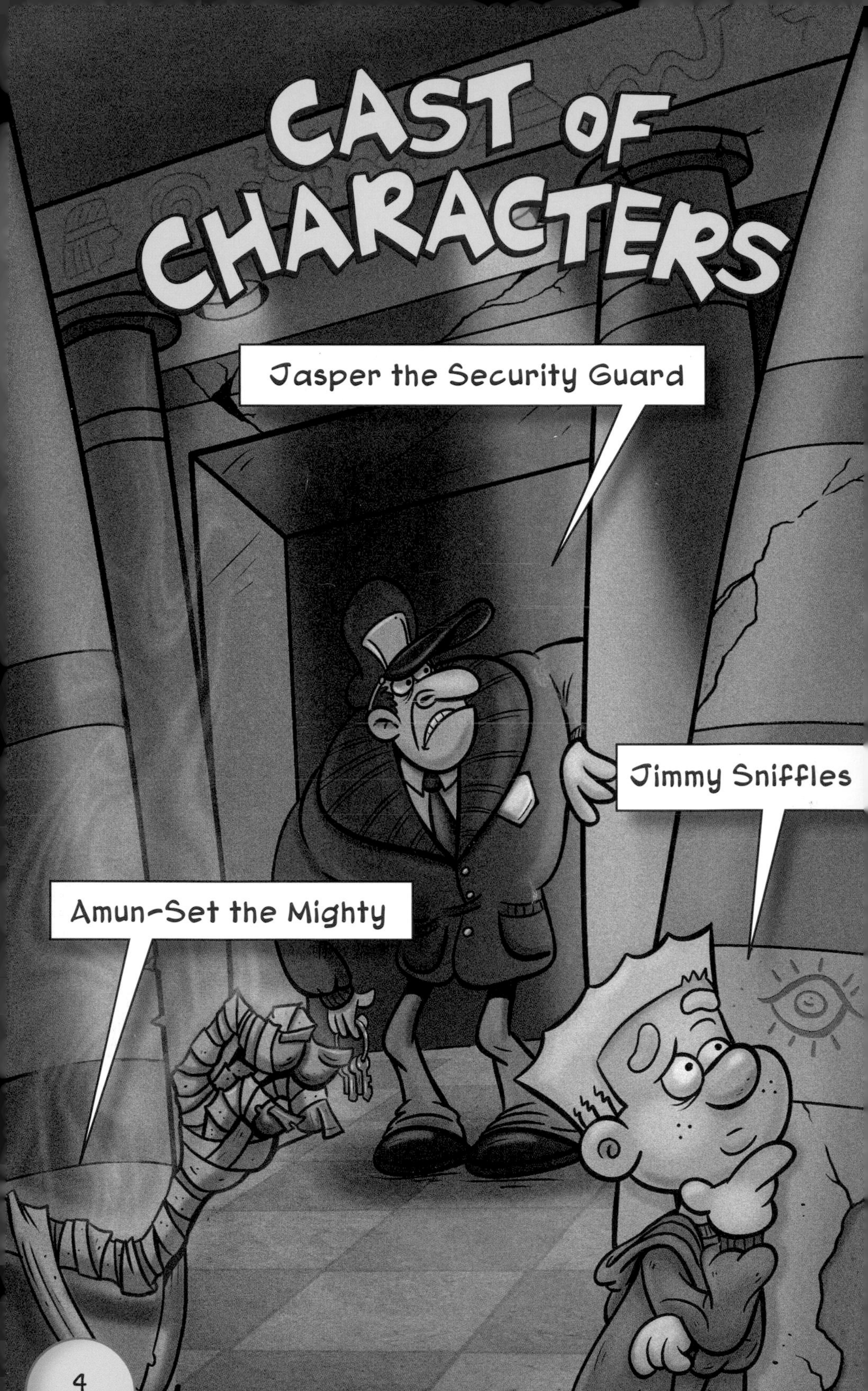
CAST OF CHARACTERS
Jasper the Security Guard
Jimmy Sniffles
Amun-Set the Mighty

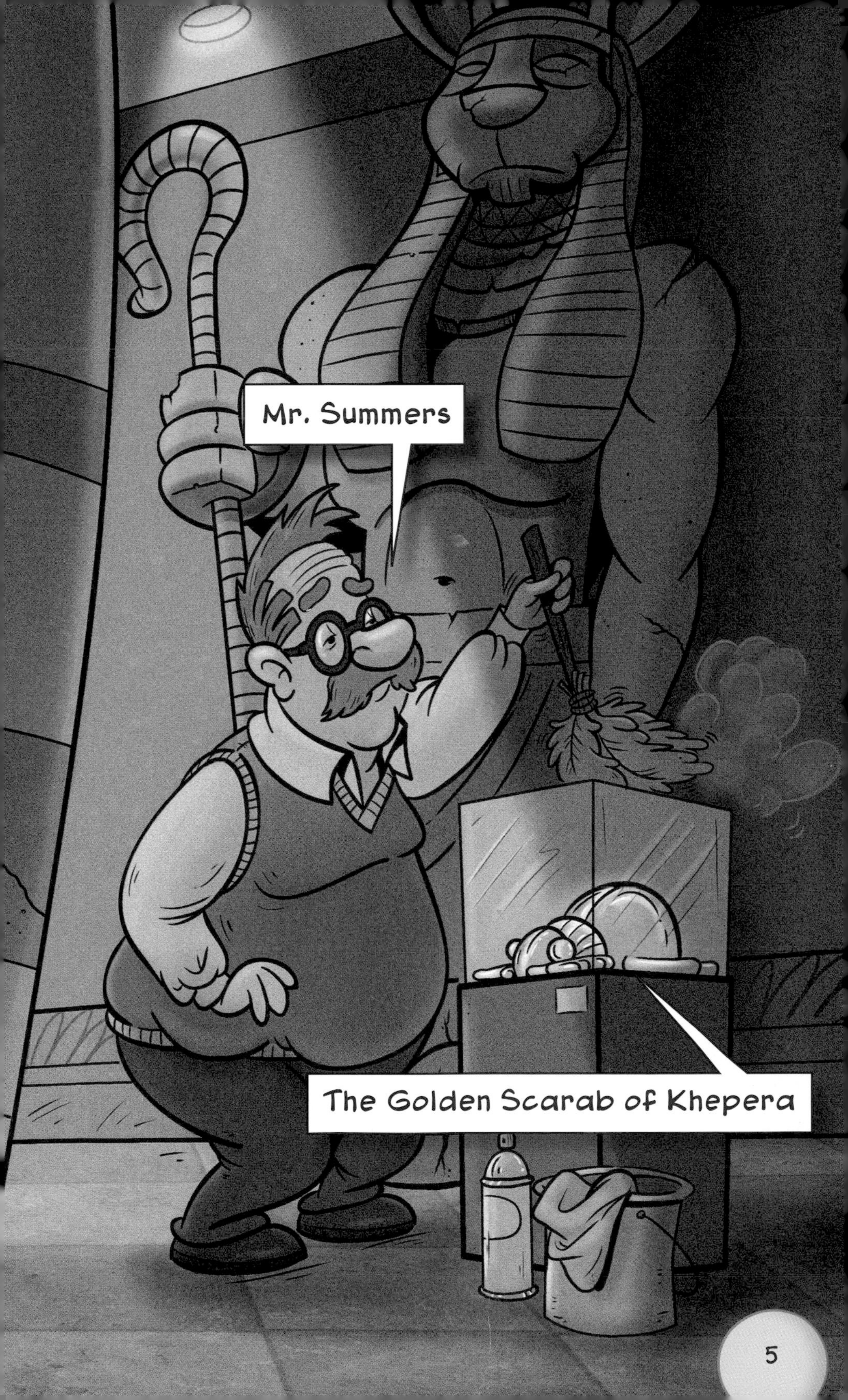
Mr. Summers
The Golden Scarab of Khepera

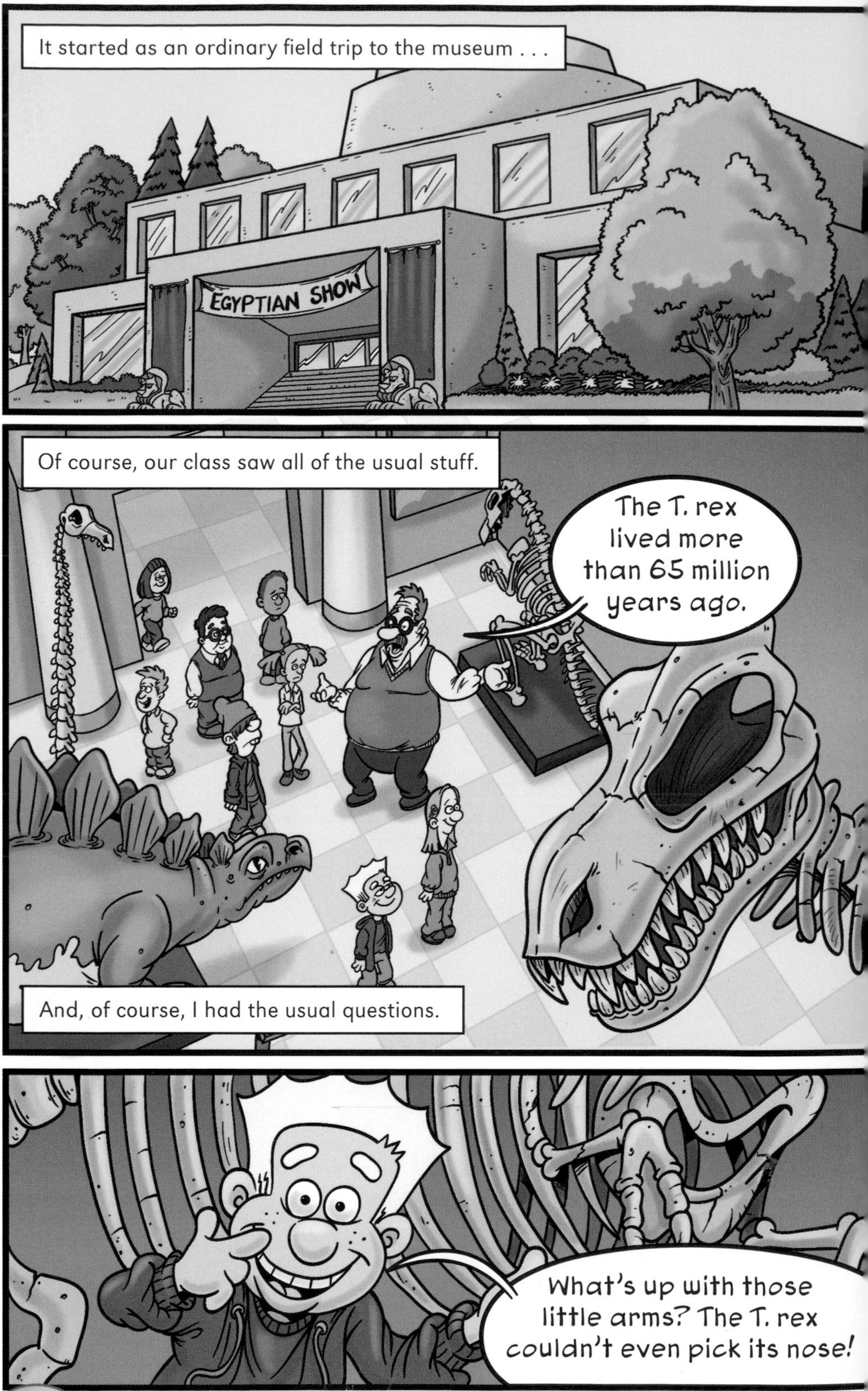
It started as an ordinary field trip to the museum . . .
EGYPTIAN SHOW
Of course, our class saw all of the usual stuff.
The T. rex lived more than 65 million years ago.
And, of course, I had the usual questions.
What's up with those little arms? The T. rex couldn't even pick its nose!

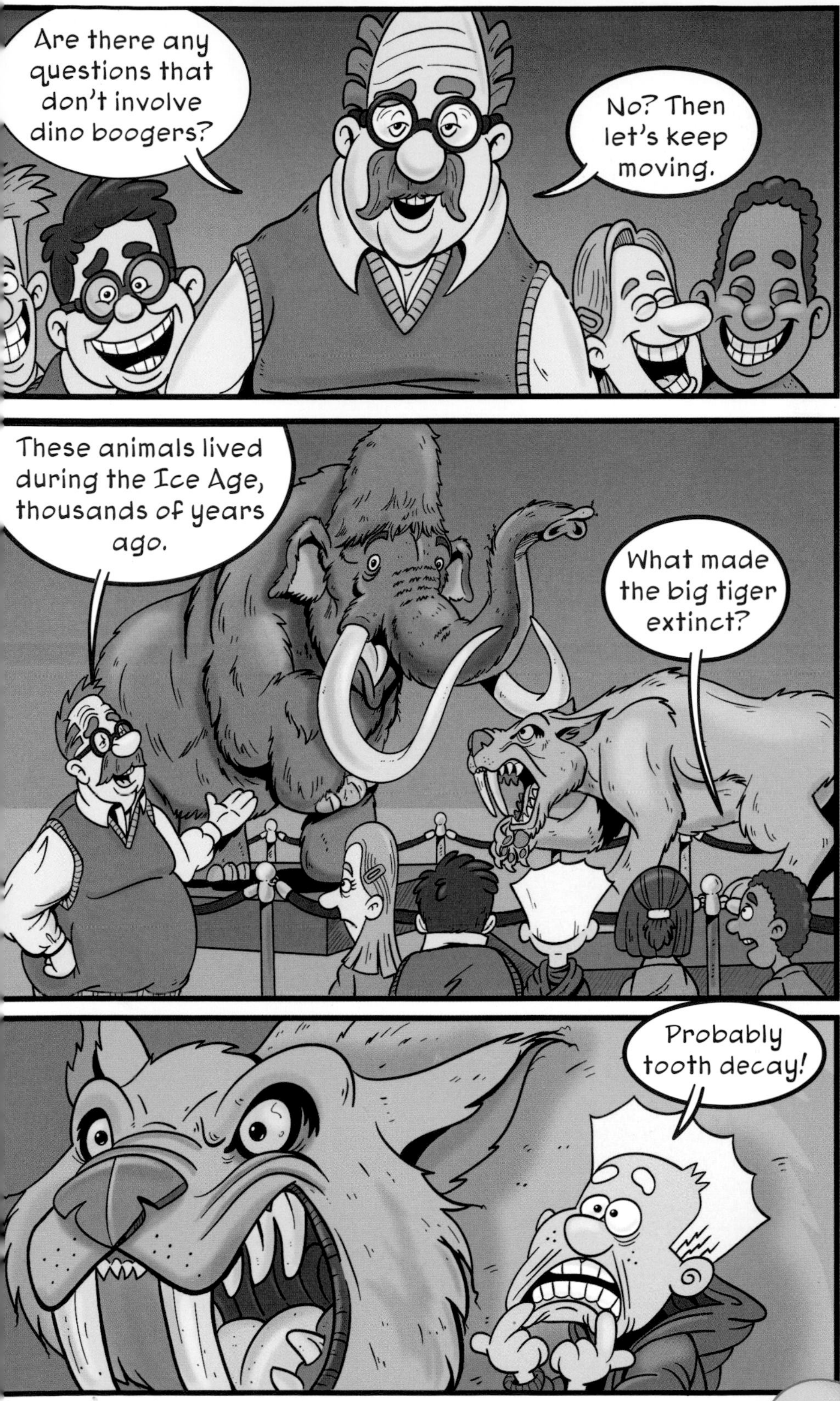
Are there any questions that don't involve dino boogers?
No? Then let's keep moving.
These animals lived during the Ice Age, thousands of years ago.
What made the big tiger extinct?
Probably tooth decay!

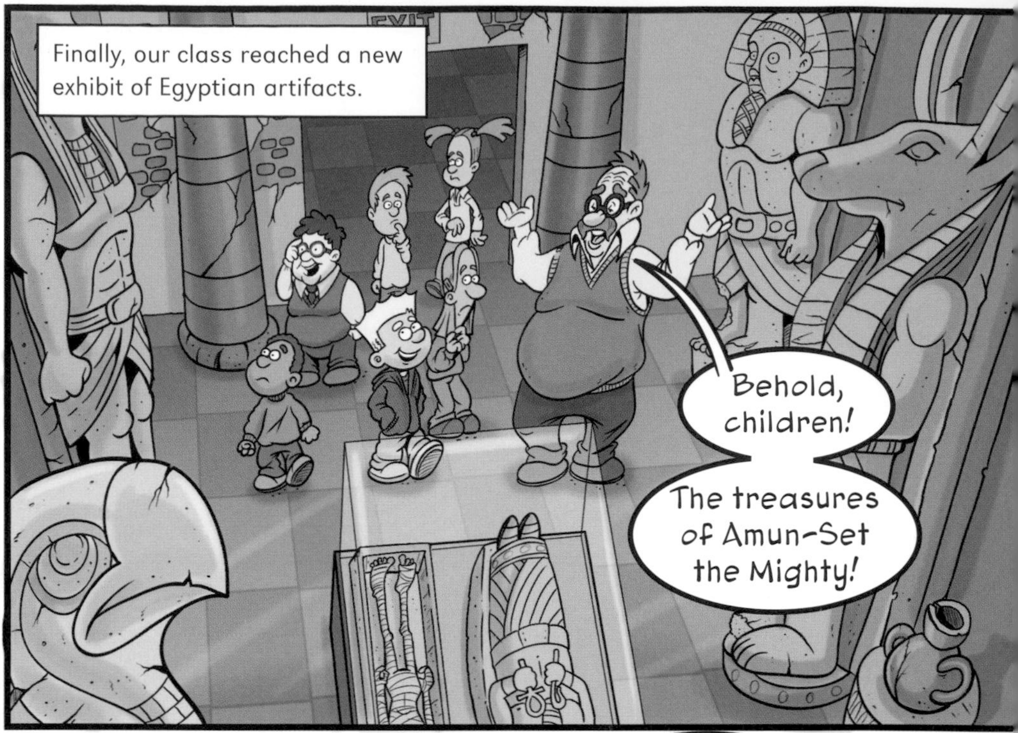
Finally, our class reached a new exhibit of Egyptian artifacts.
Behold, children!
The treasures of Amun-Set the Mighty!

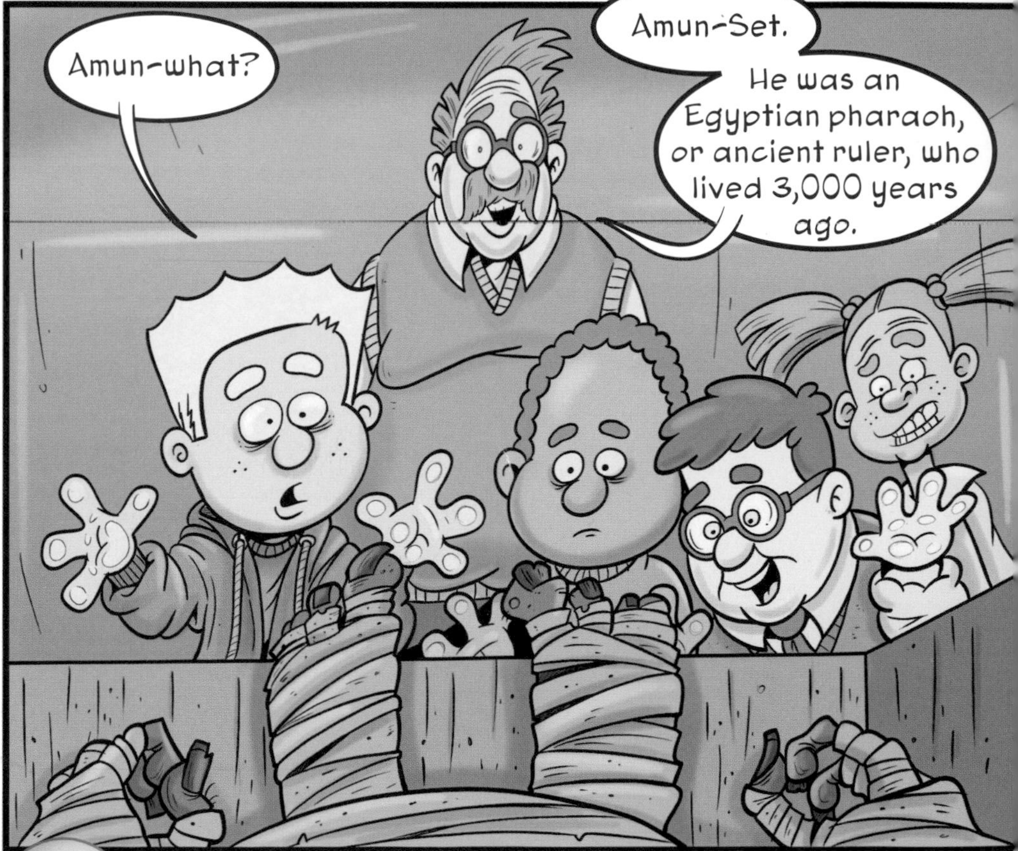
Amun-what?
Amun-Set.
He was an Egyptian pharaoh, or ancient ruler, who lived 3,000 years ago.

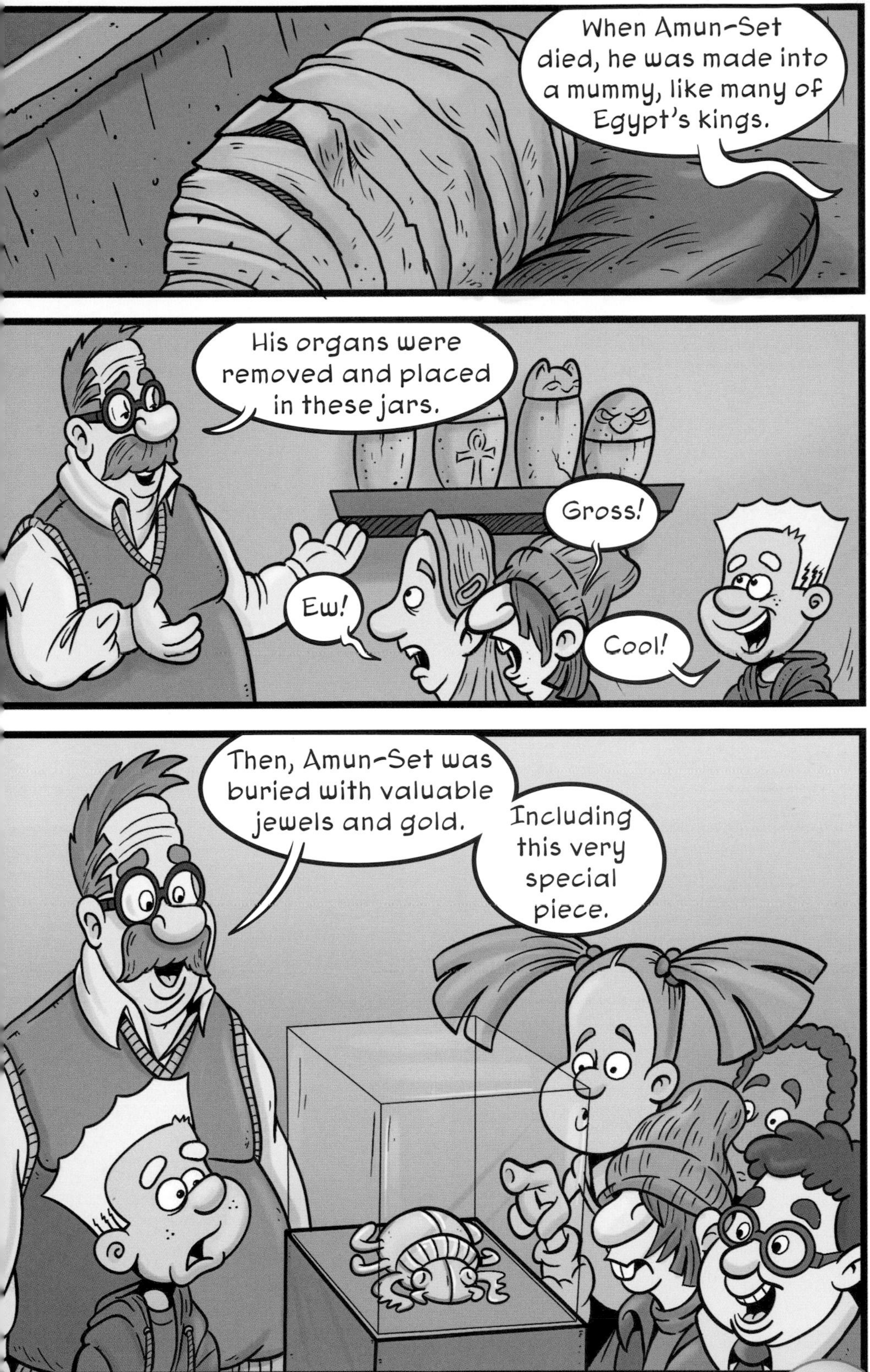
When Amun-Set died, he was made into a mummy, like many of Egypt's kings.
His organs were removed and placed in these jars.
Ew!
Gross!
Cool!
Then, Amun-Set was buried with valuable jewels and gold.
Including this very special piece.

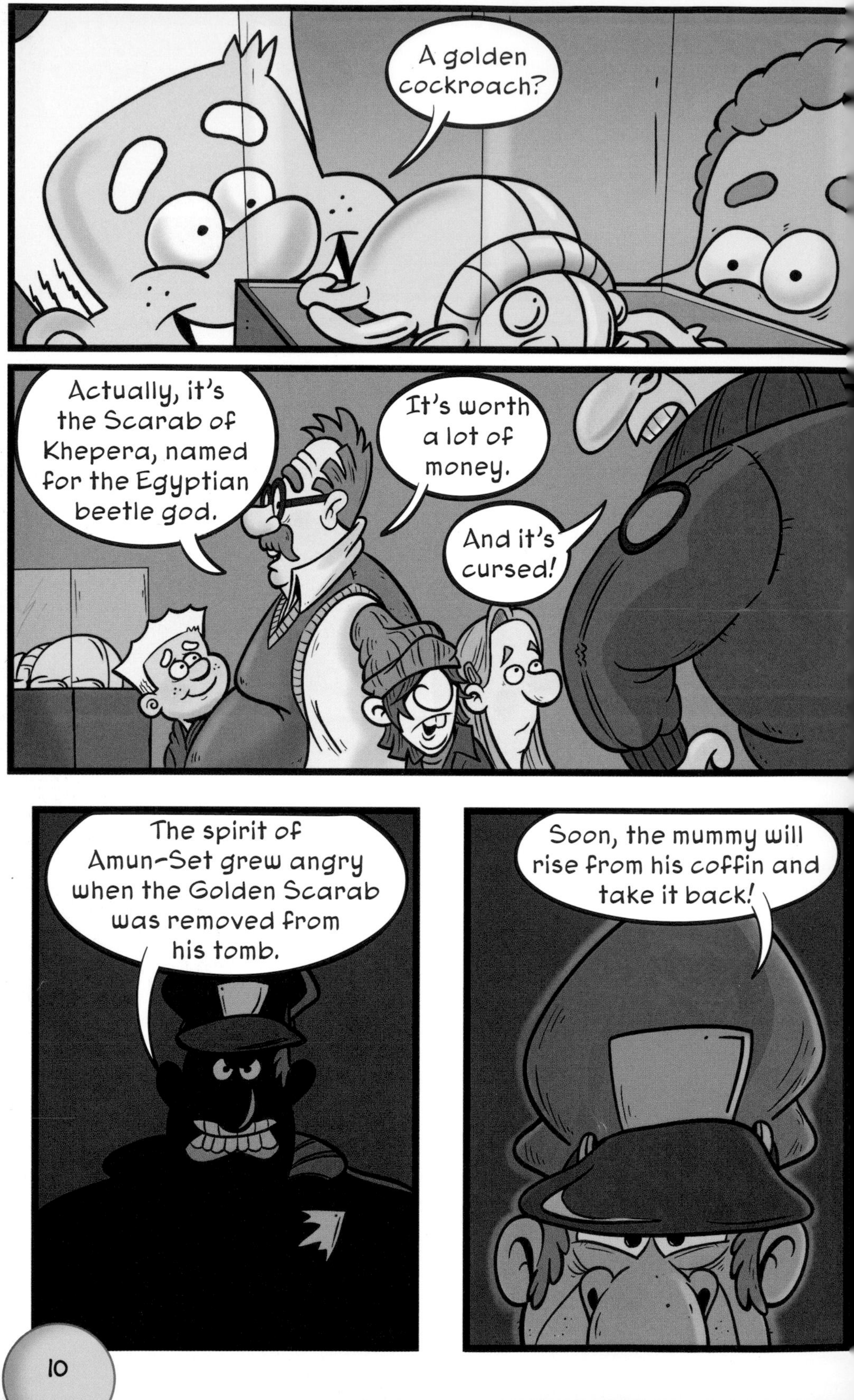
A golden cockroach?
Actually, it's the Scarab of Khepera, named for the Egyptian beetle god.
It's worth a lot of money.
And it's cursed!
The spirit of Amun-Set grew angry when the Golden Scarab was removed from his tomb.
Soon, the mummy will rise from his coffin and take it back!

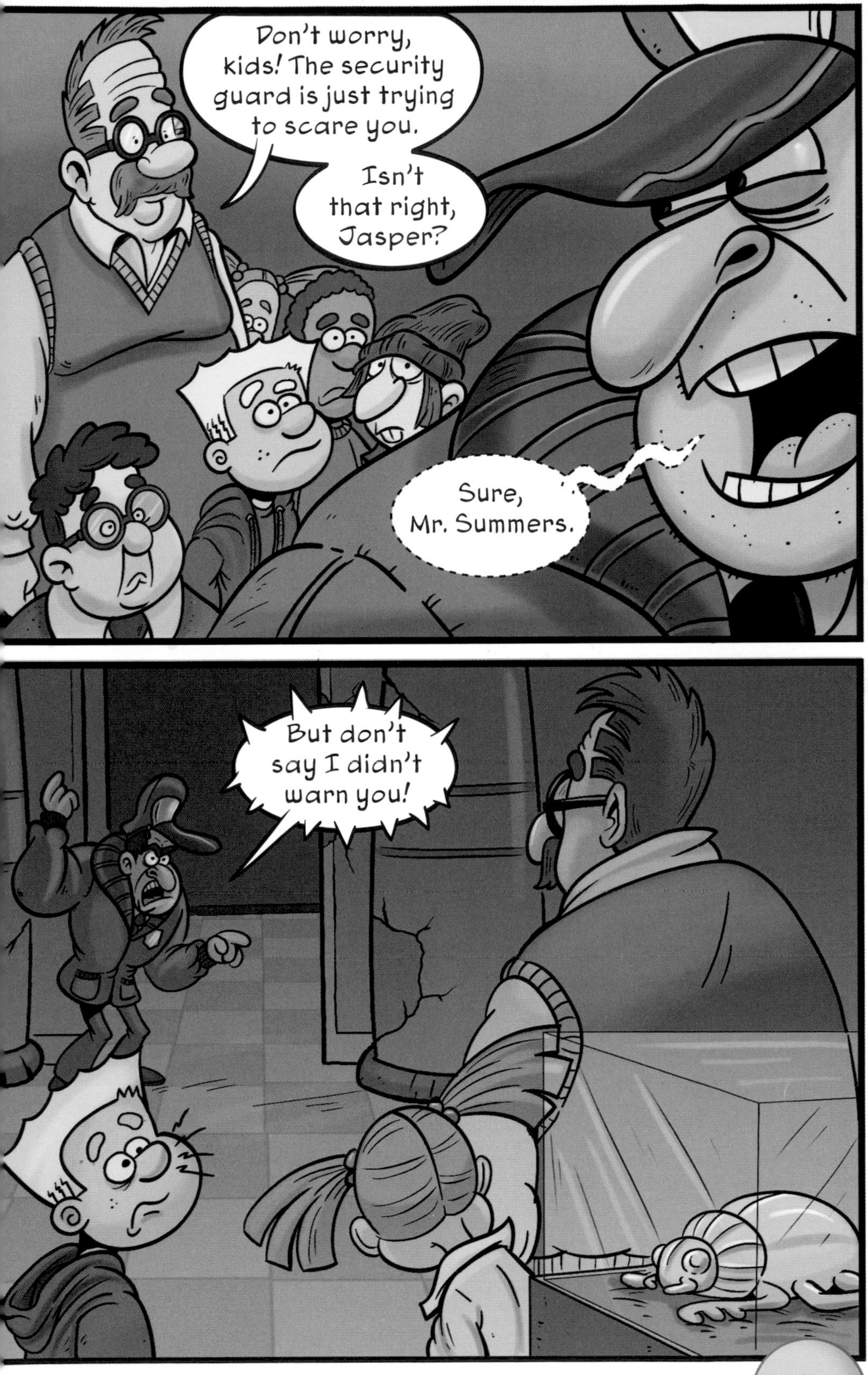
Don't worry, kids! The security guard is just trying to scare you.
Isn't that right, Jasper?
Sure, Mr. Summers.
But don't say I didn't warn you!

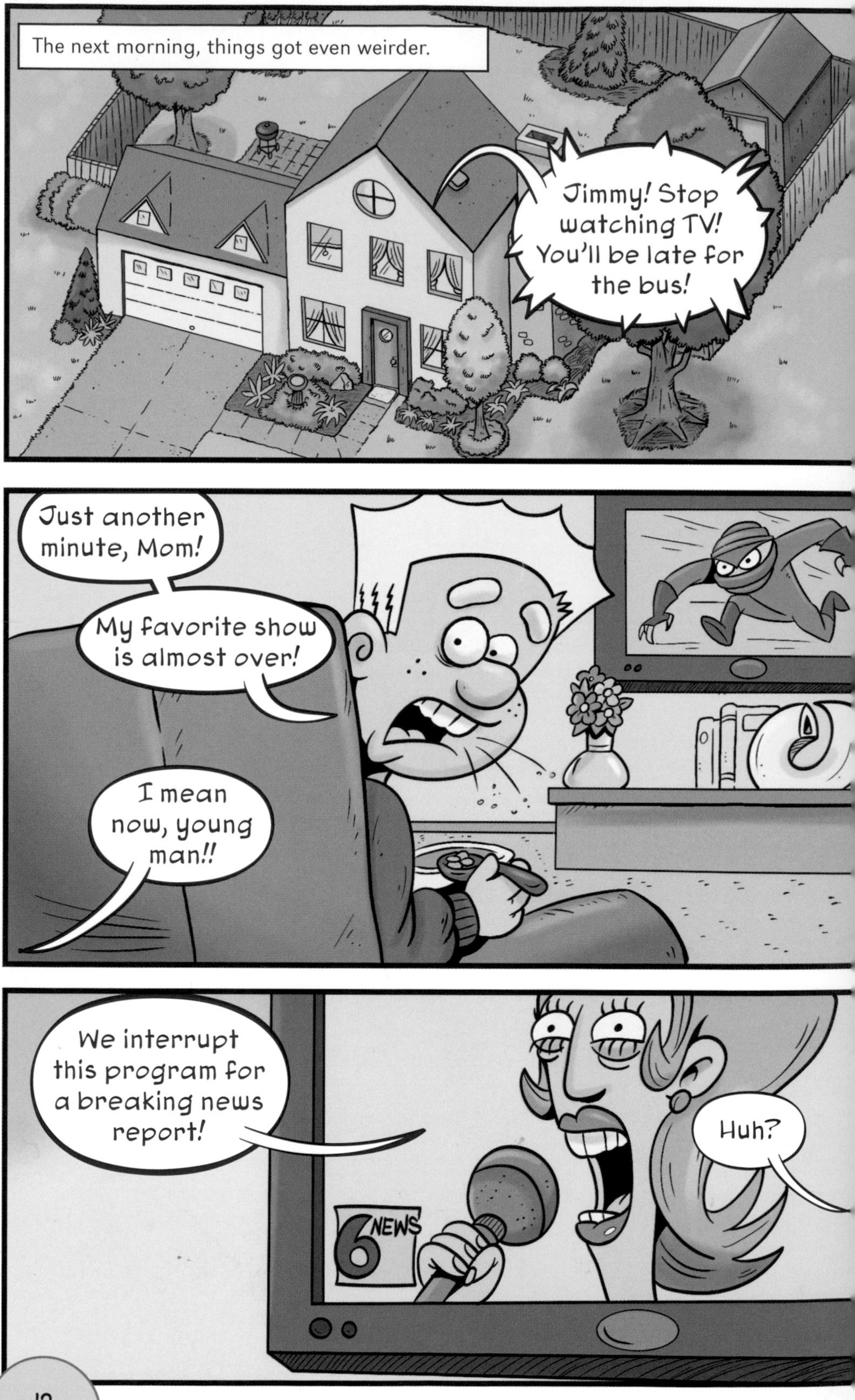
The next morning, things got even weirder.
Jimmy! Stop watching TV! You'll be late for the bus!
Just another minute, Mom!
My favorite show is almost over!
I mean now, young man!!
We interrupt this program for a breaking news report!
Huh?
6 NEWS

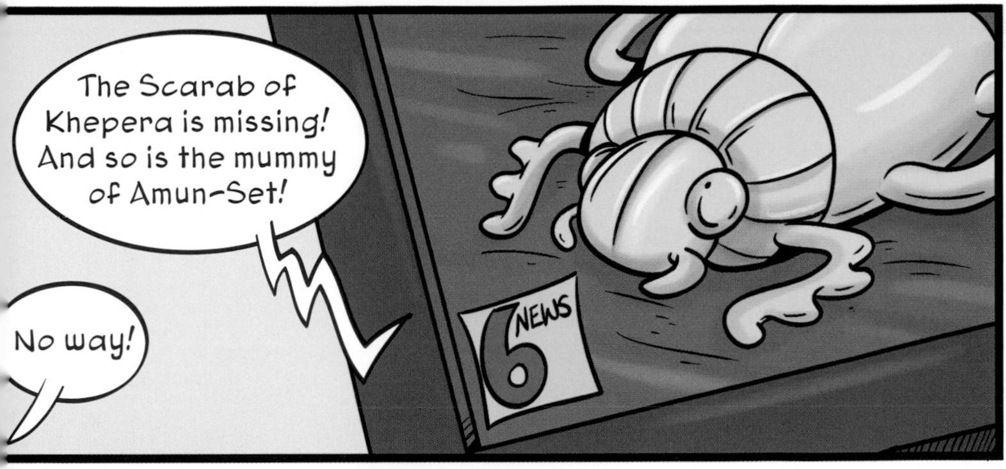
The Scarab of Khepera is missing! And so is the mummy of Amun-Set!
No way!
NEWS 6

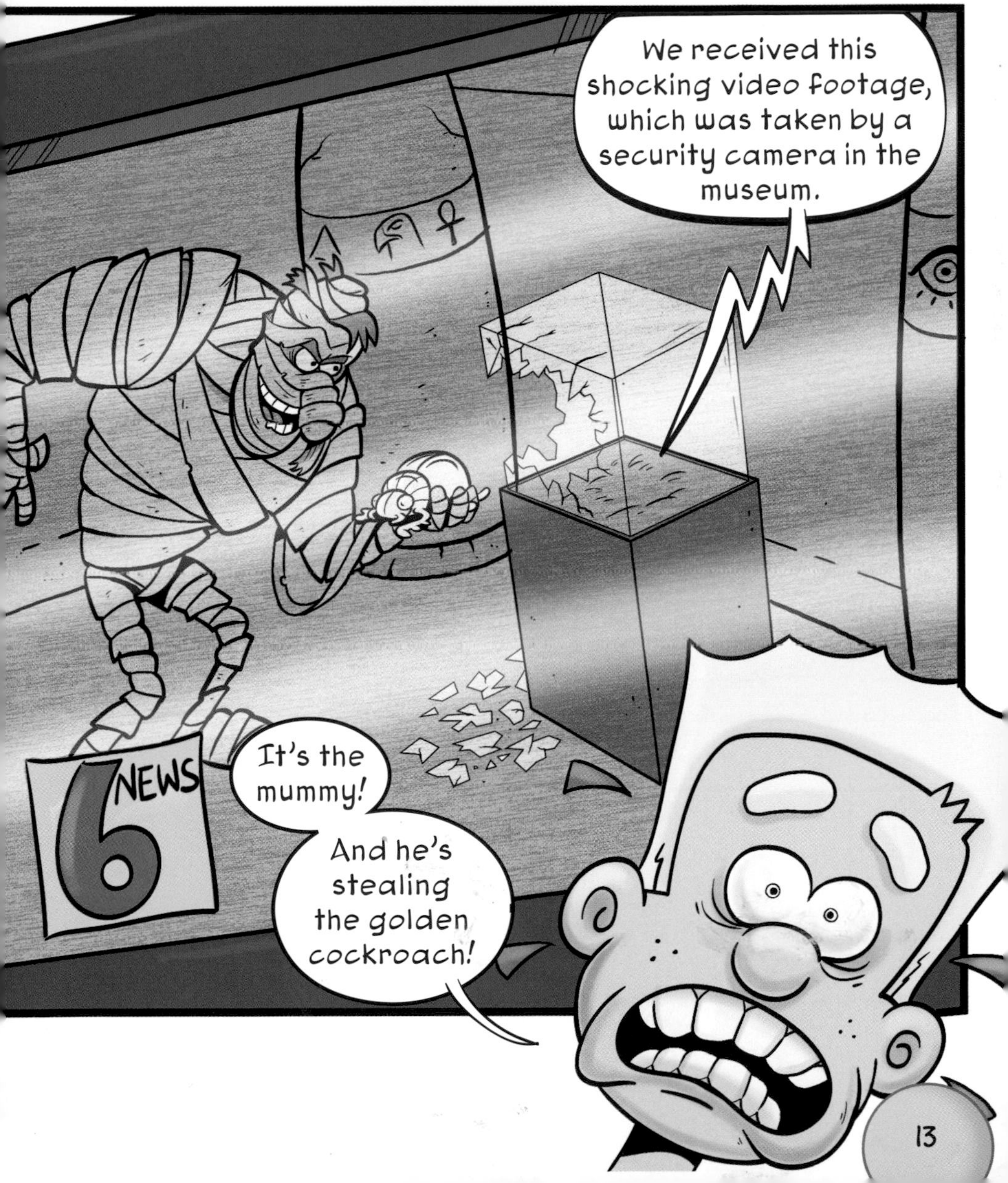
We received this shocking video footage, which was taken by a security camera in the museum.
NEWS 6
It's the mummy!
And he's stealing the golden cockroach!

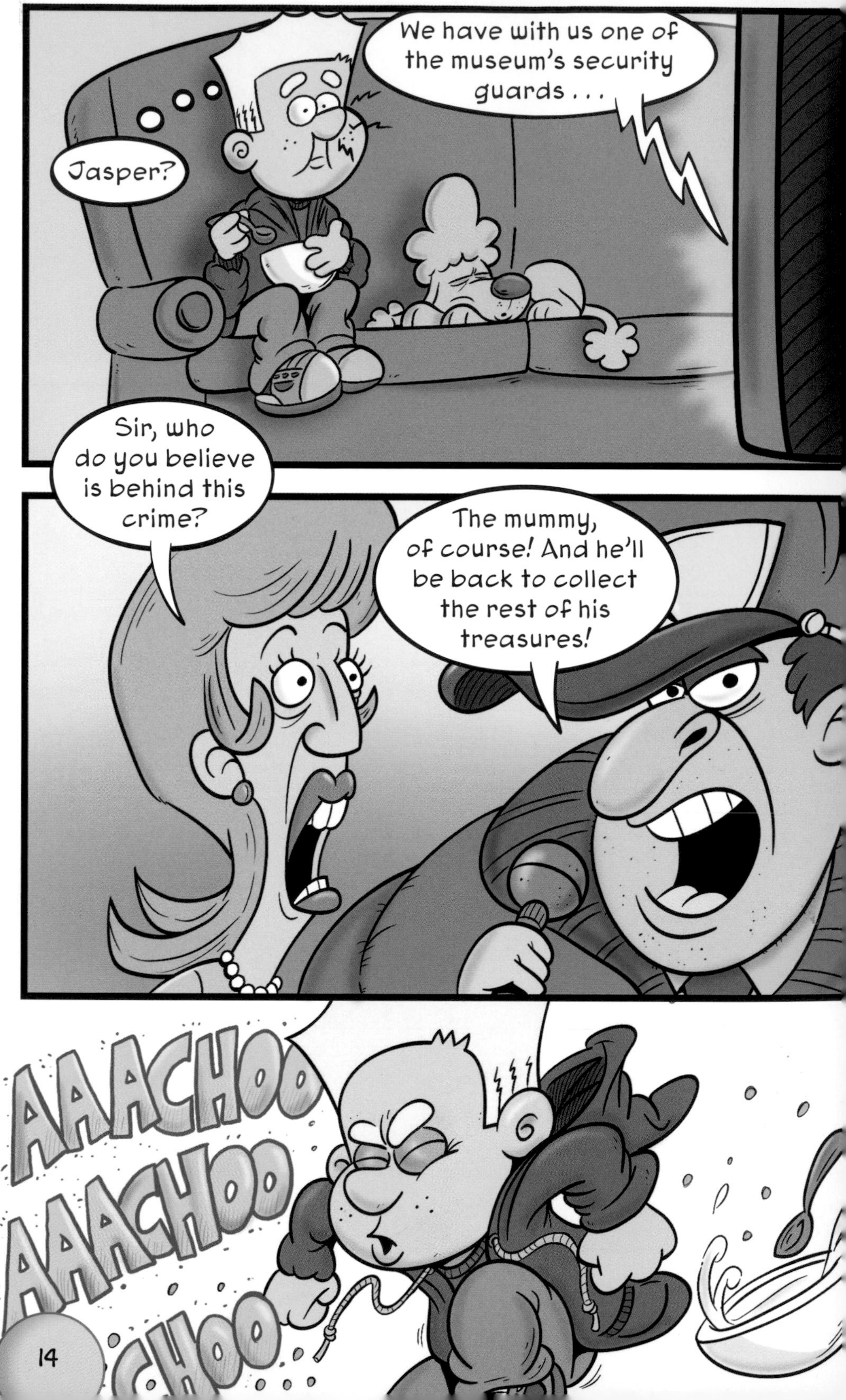
We have with us one of the museum's security guards . . .
Jasper?
Sir, who do you believe is behind this crime?
The mummy, of course! And he'll be back to collect the rest of his treasures!
AAACHOO
AAACHOO
CHOO

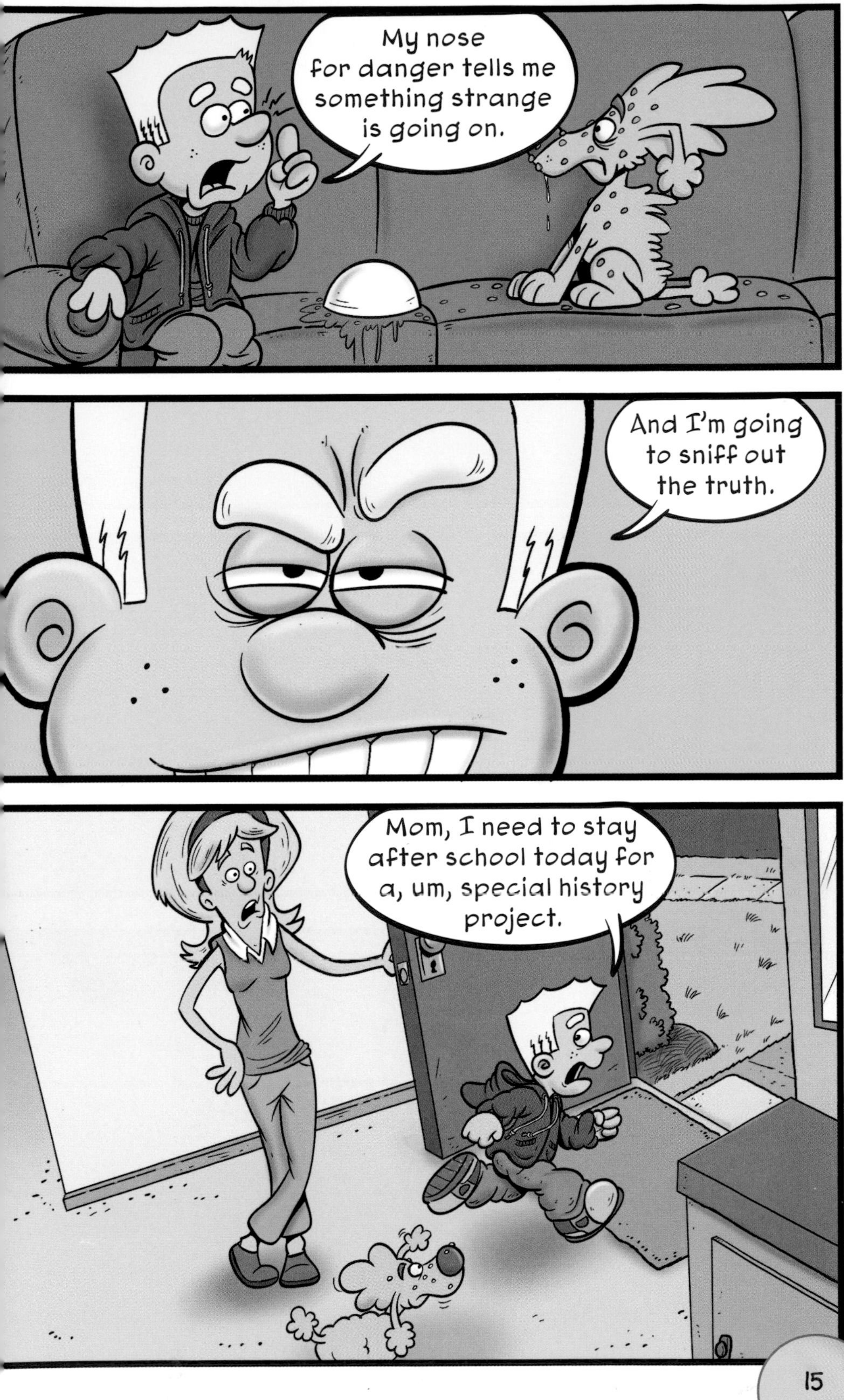
My nose for danger tells me something strange is going on.
And I'm going to sniff out the truth.
Mom, I need to stay after school today for a, um, special history project.

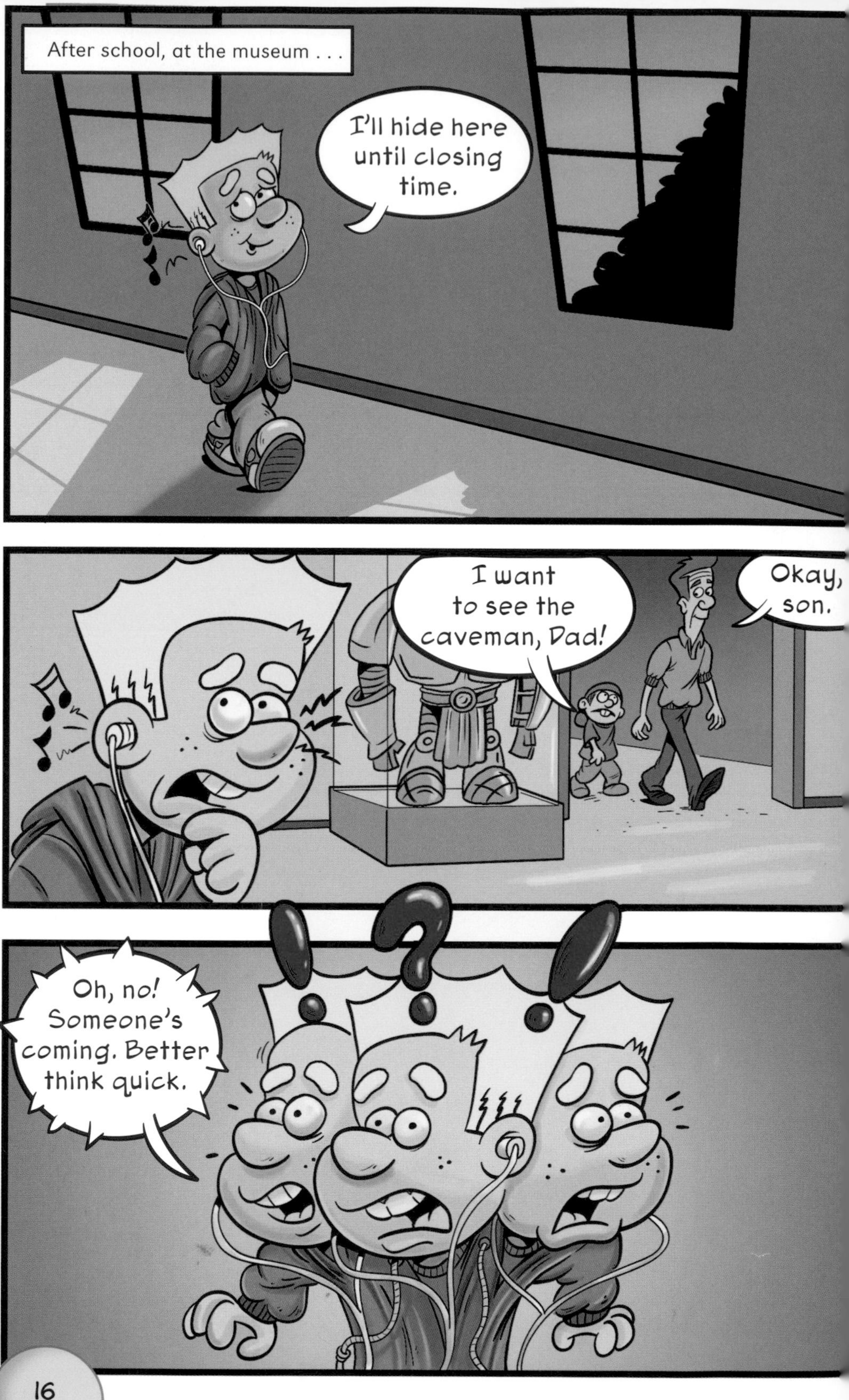
After school, at the museum . . .
I'll hide here until closing time.
I want to see the caveman, Dad!
Okay, son.
Oh, no! Someone's coming. Better think quick.

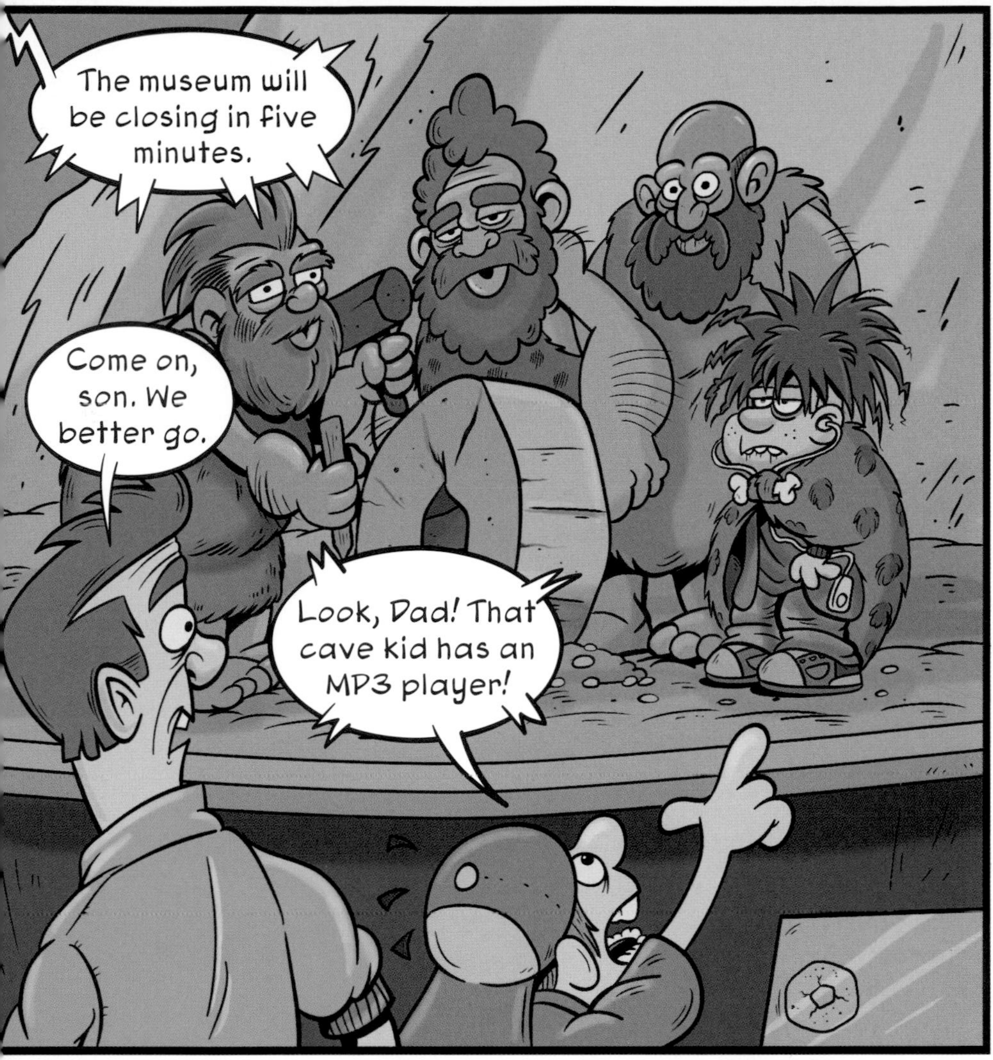
The museum will be closing in five minutes.
Come on, son. We better go.
Look, Dad! That cave kid has an MP3 player!

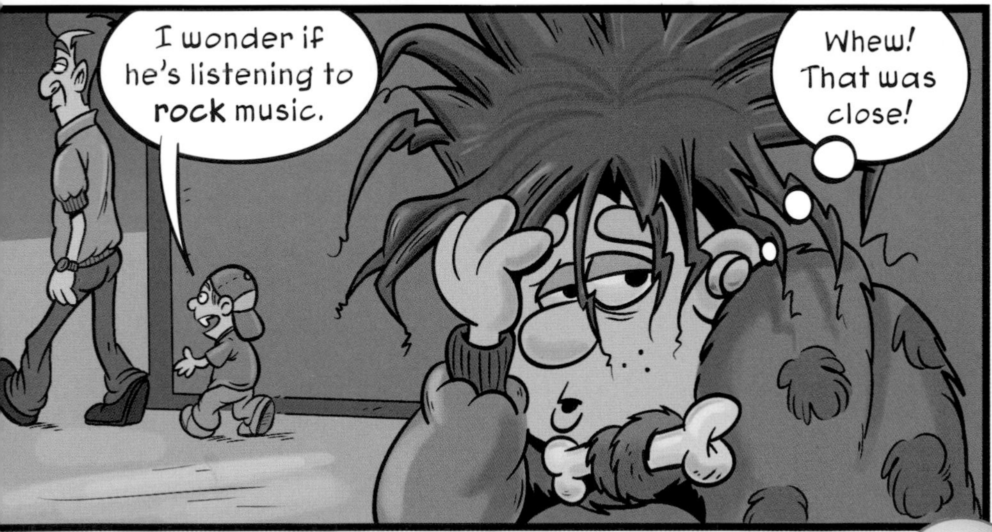
I wonder if he's listening to **rock** music.
Whew! That was close!

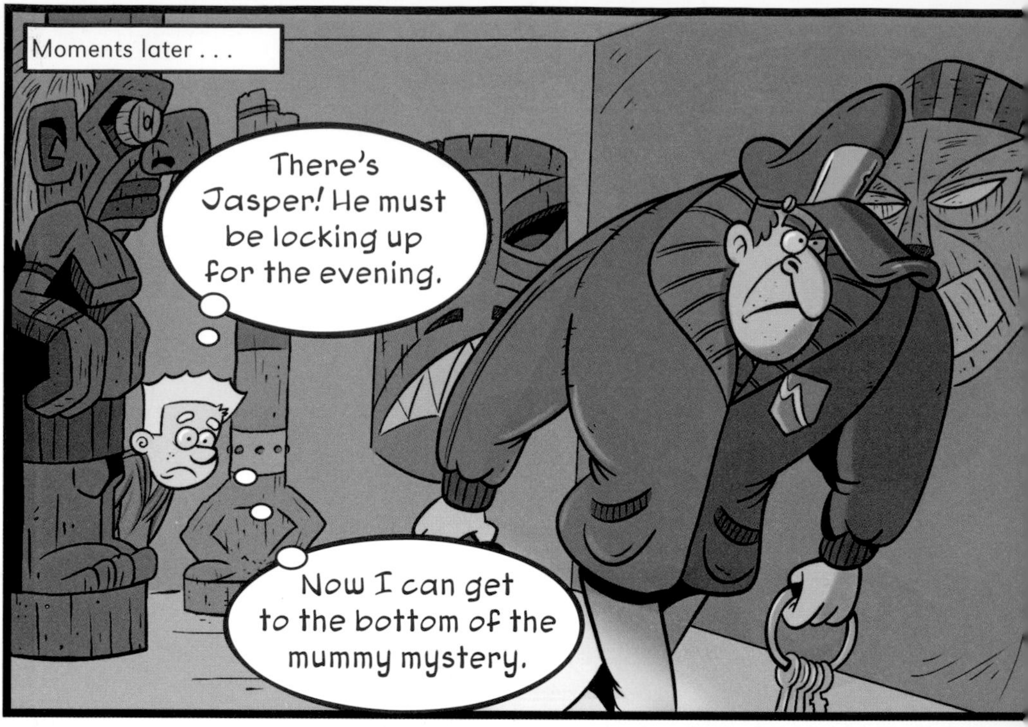
Moments later . . .
There's Jasper! He must be locking up for the evening.
Now I can get to the bottom of the mummy mystery.

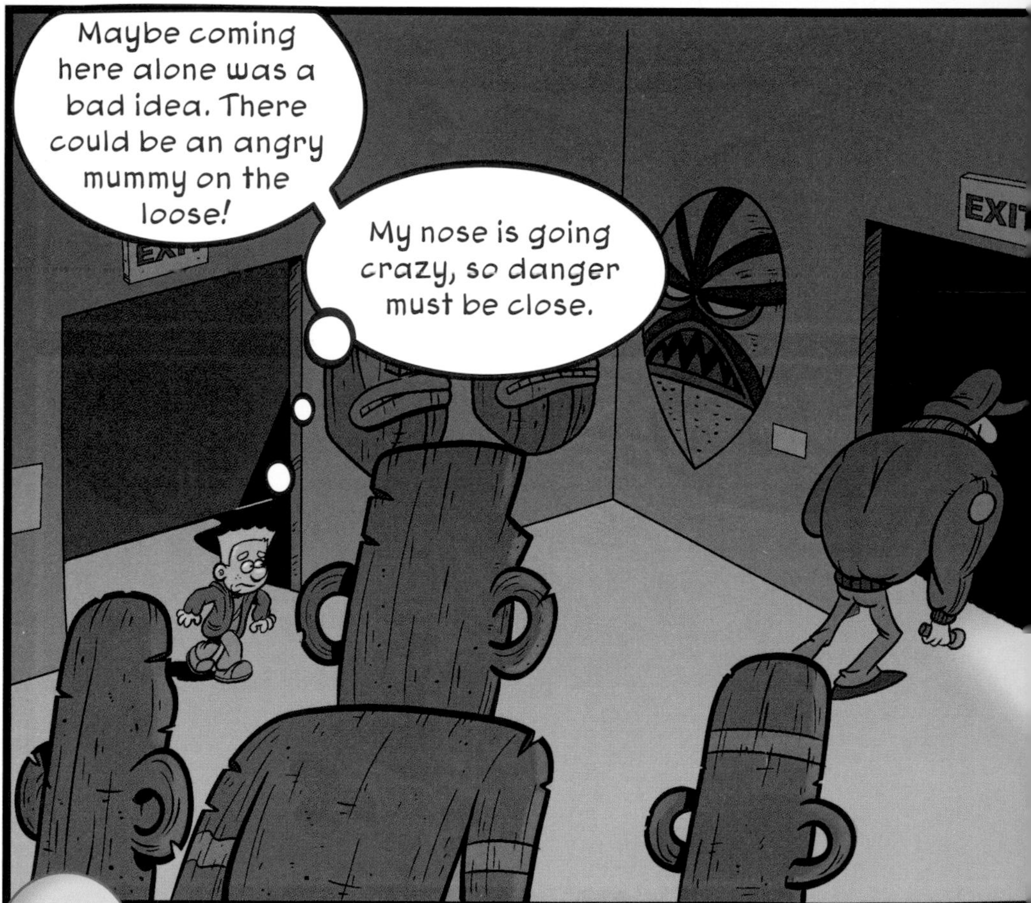
Maybe coming here alone was a bad idea. There could be an angry mummy on the loose!
My nose is going crazy, so danger must be close.
EXIT

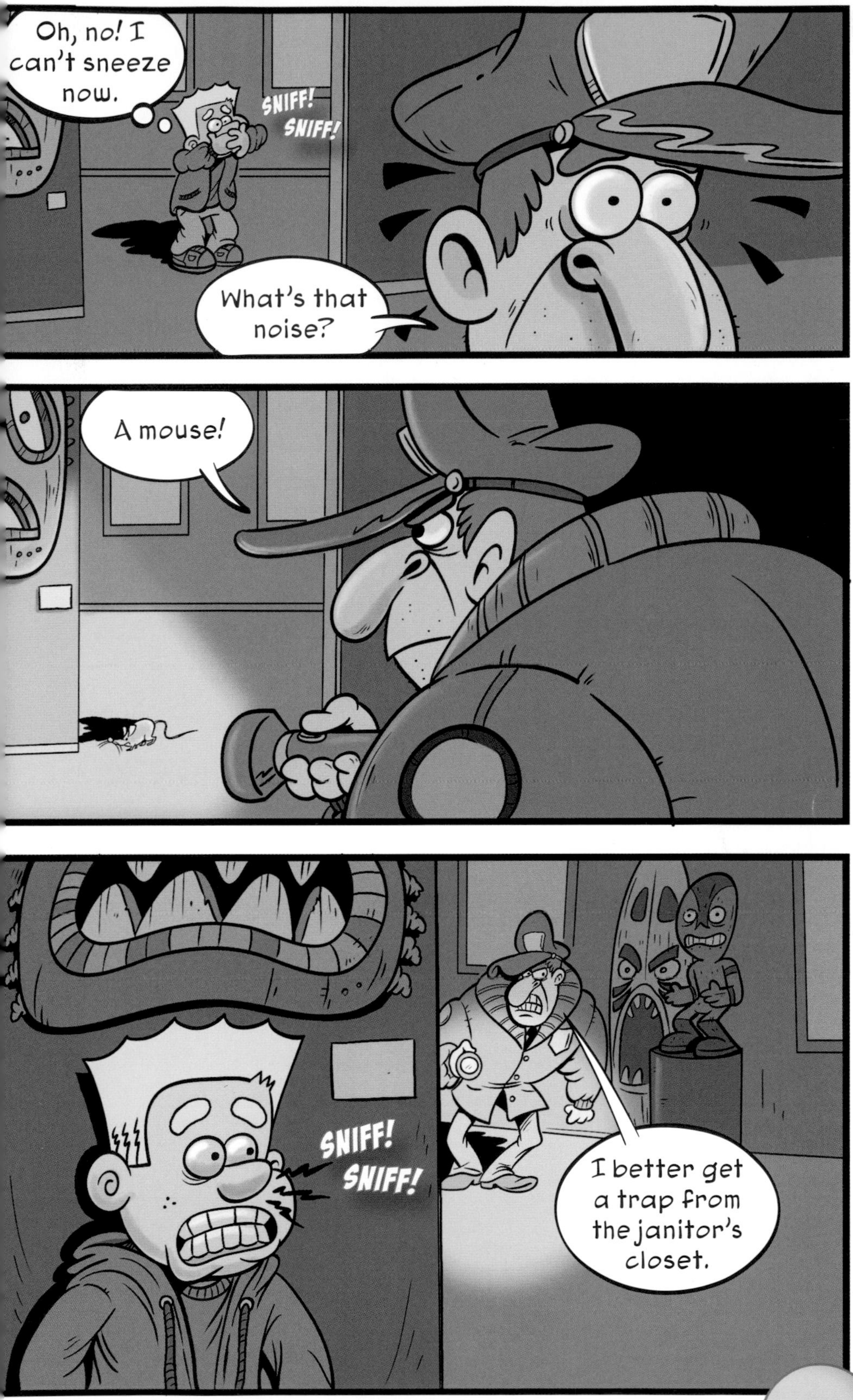

Oh, no! I can't sneeze now.
SNIFF! SNIFF!
What's that noise?
A mouse!
SNIFF! SNIFF!
I better get a trap from the janitor's closet.

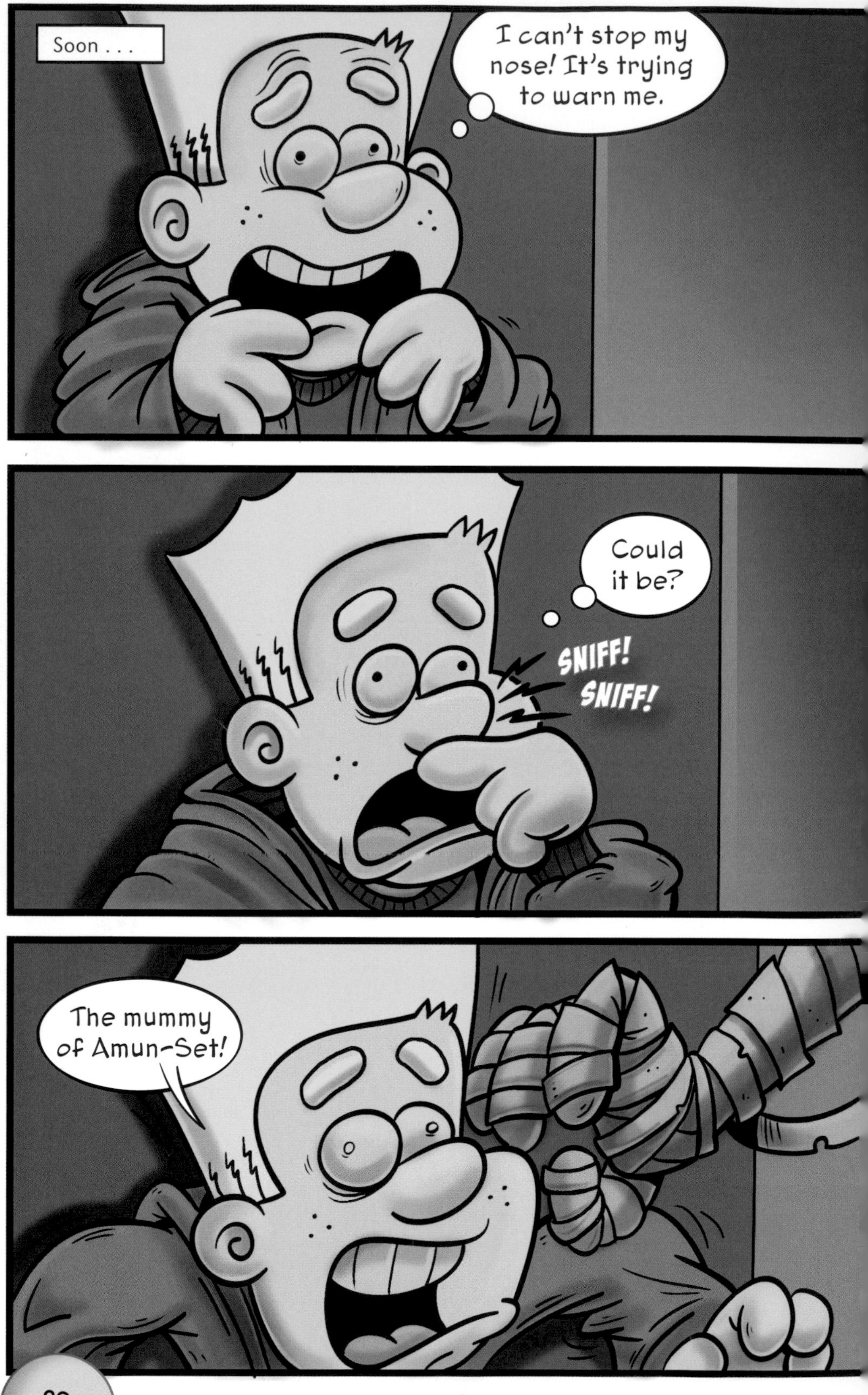
Soon . . .
I can't stop my nose! It's trying to warn me.
Could it be?
SNIFF! SNIFF!
The mummy of Amun-Set!

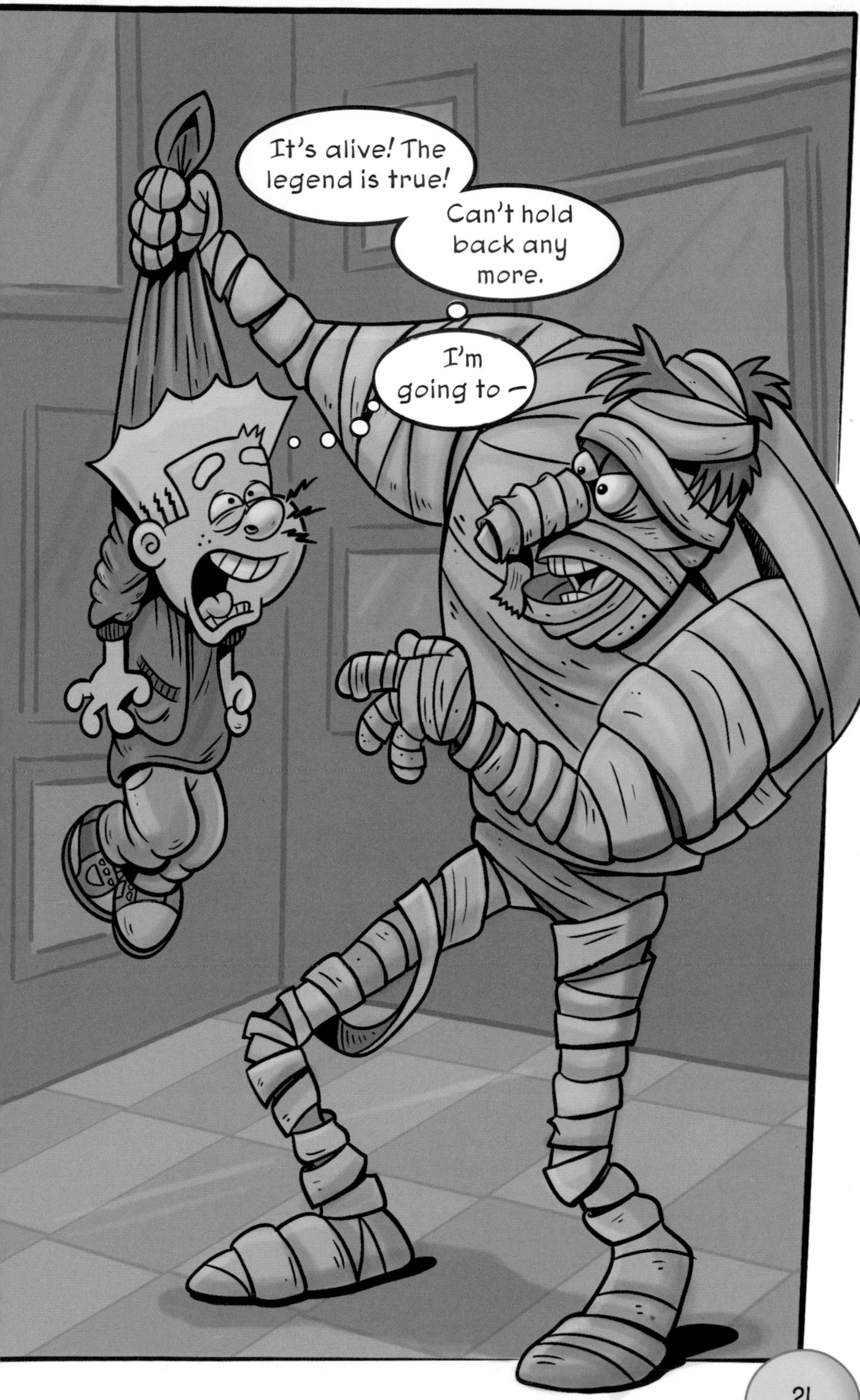
It's alive! The legend is true!
Can't hold back any more.
I'm going to —

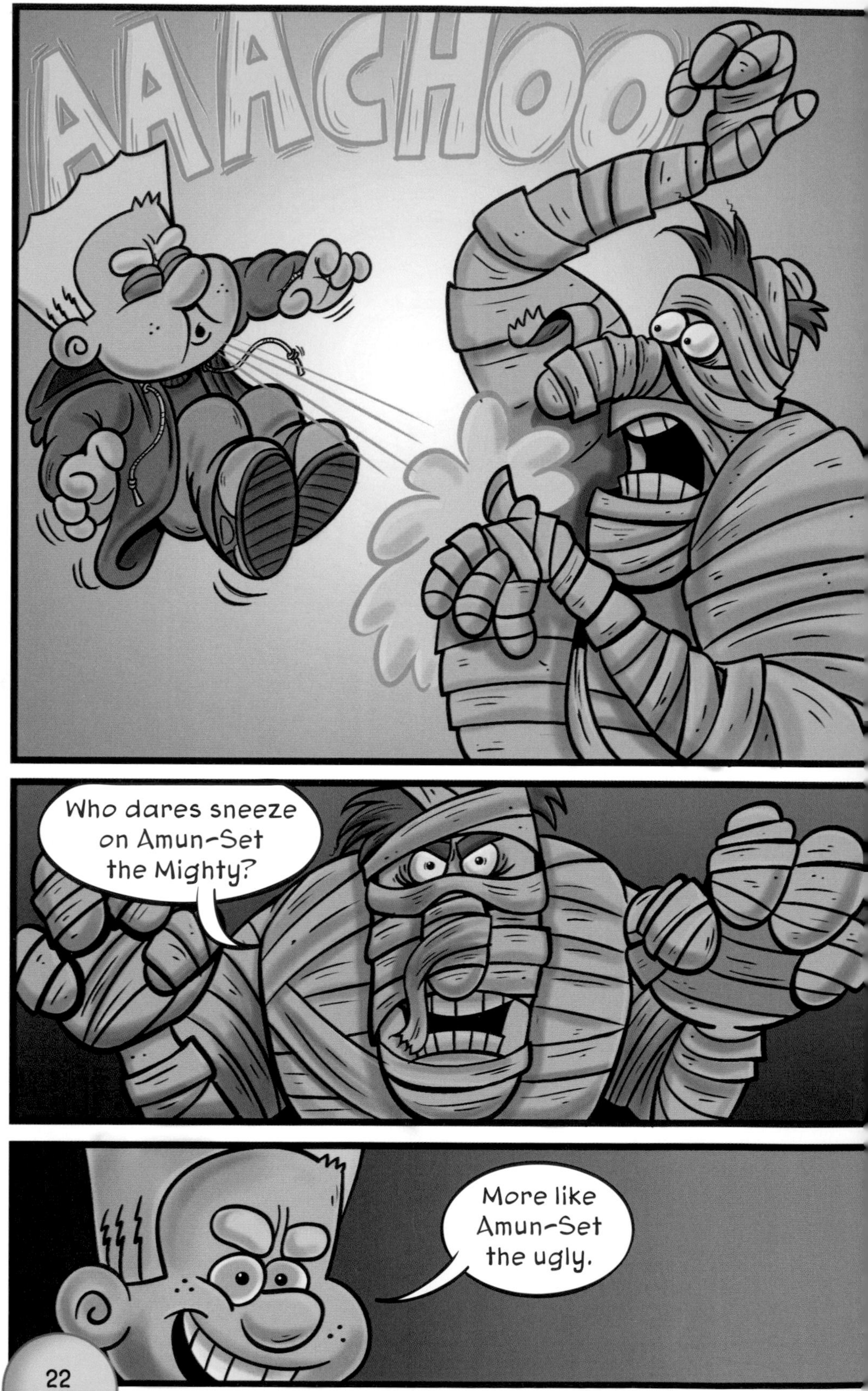
AACHOO
Who dares sneeze on Amun-Set the Mighty?
More like Amun-Set the ugly.

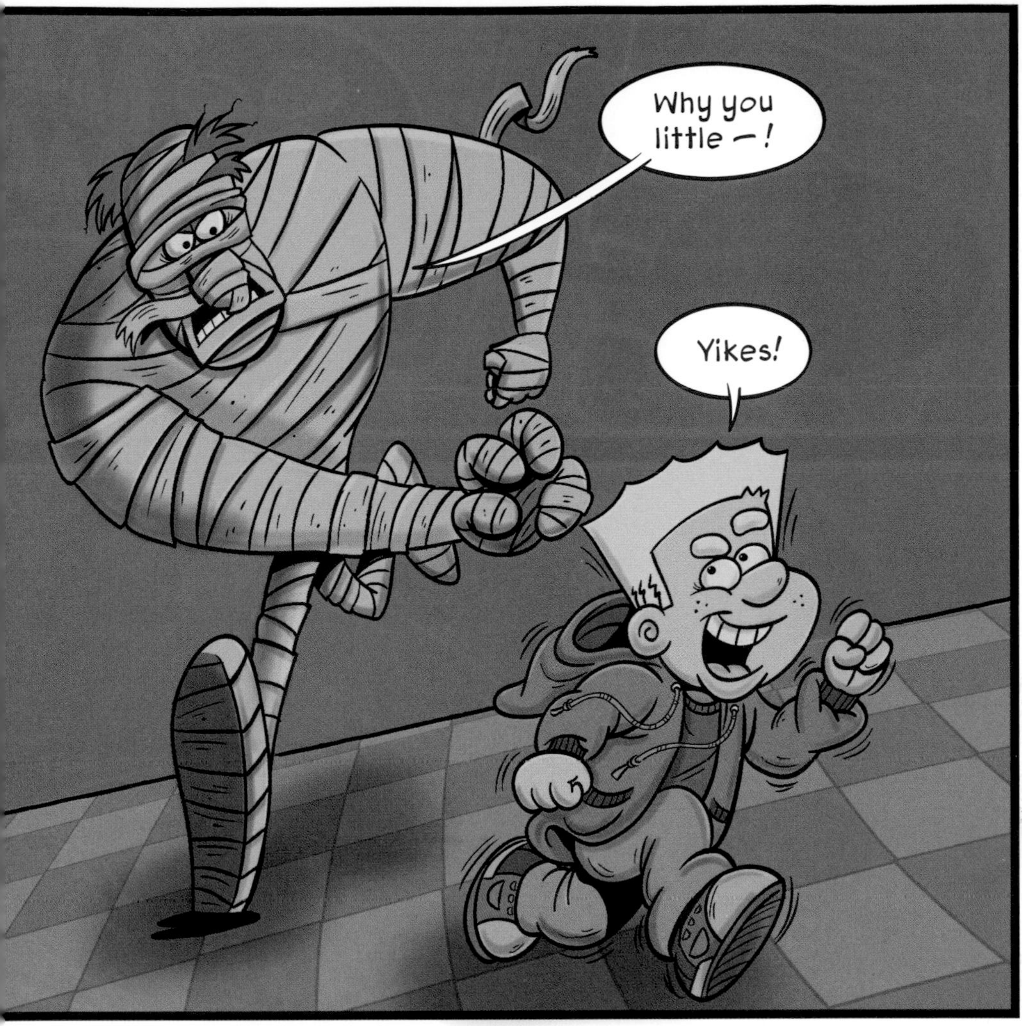
Why you little —!
Yikes!

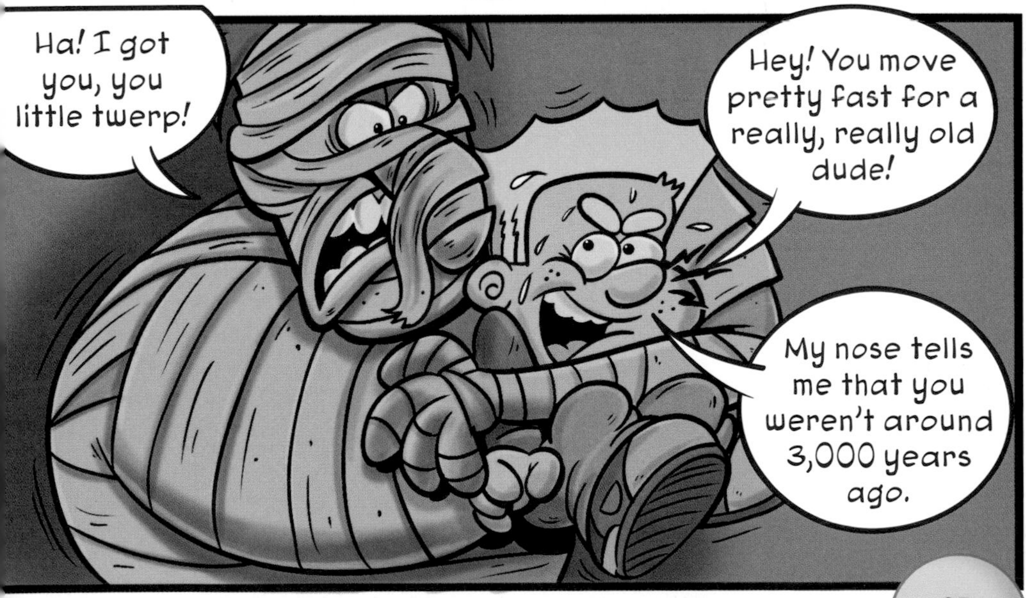
Ha! I got you, you little twerp!
Hey! You move pretty fast for a really, really old dude!
My nose tells me that you weren't around 3,000 years ago.

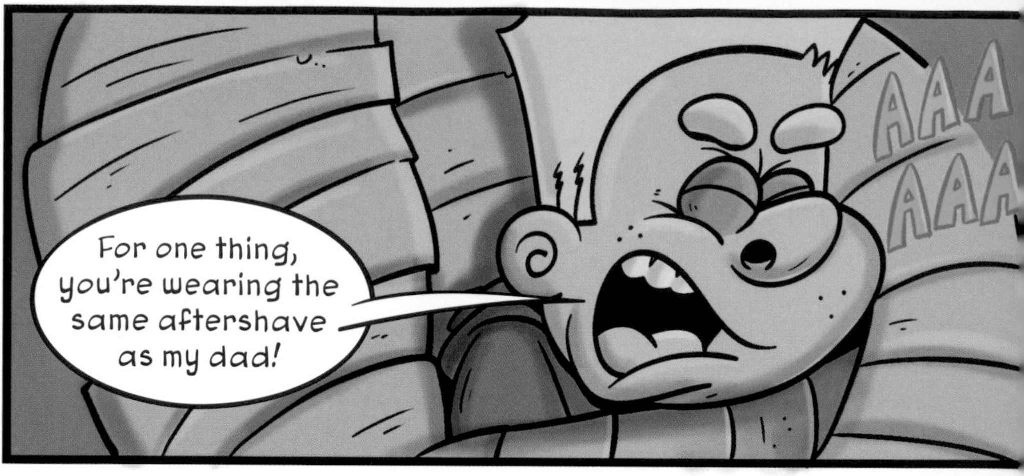
For one thing, you're wearing the same aftershave as my dad!
AAA AAA

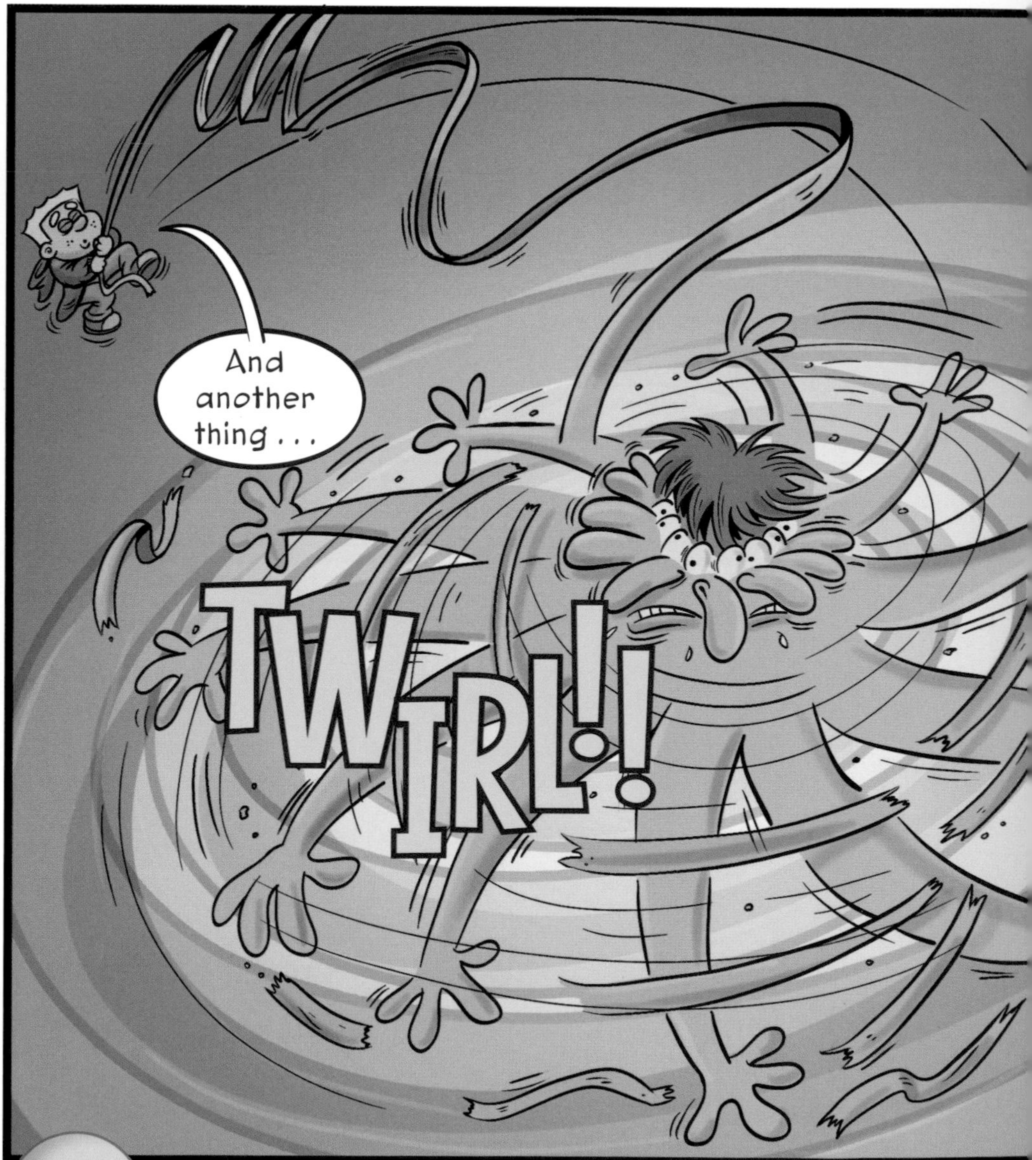
And another thing . . .
TWIRL!!

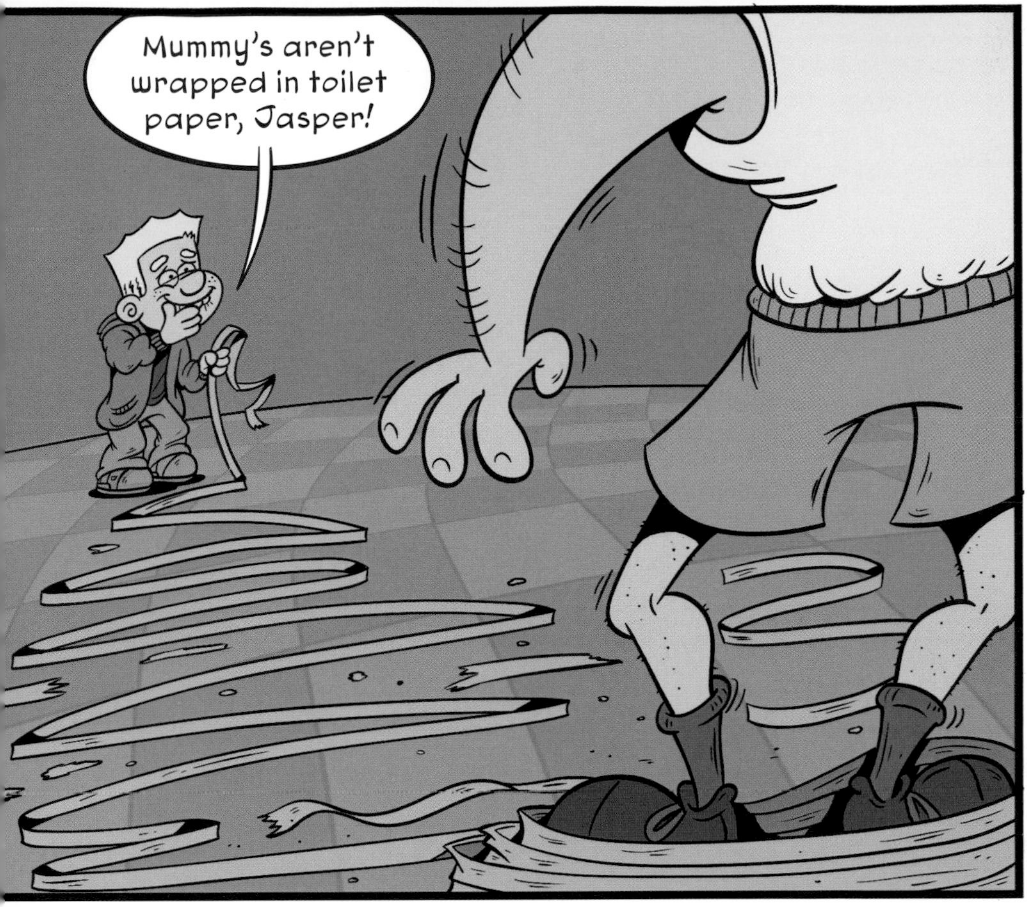
Mummy's aren't wrapped in toilet paper, Jasper!

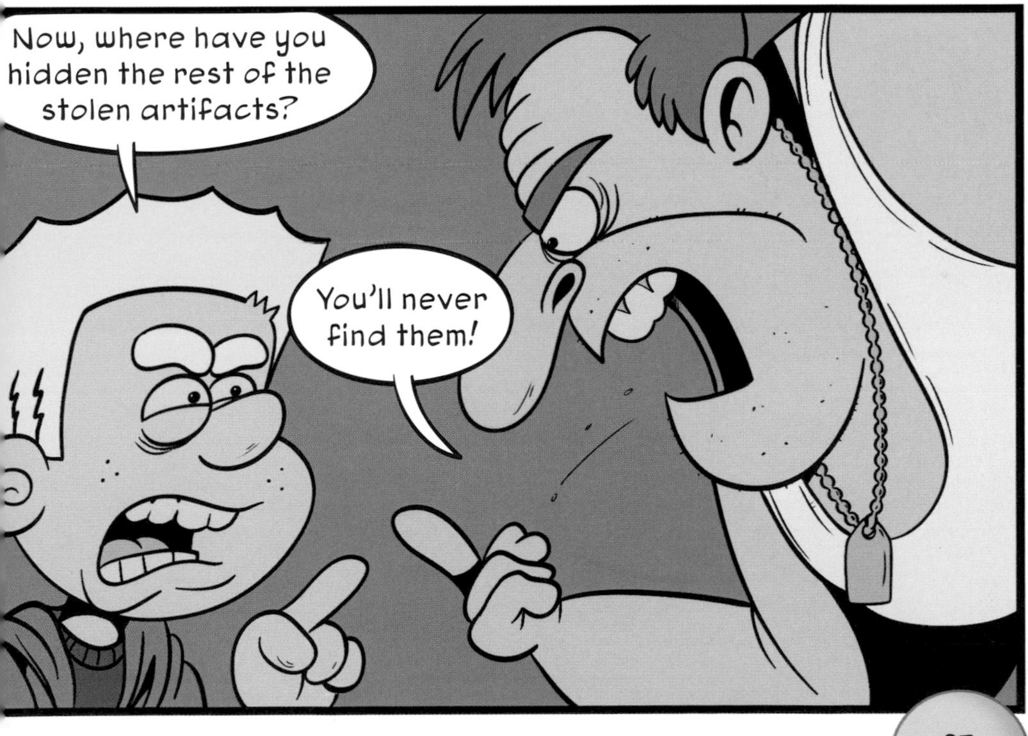
Now, where have you hidden the rest of the stolen artifacts?
You'll never find them!

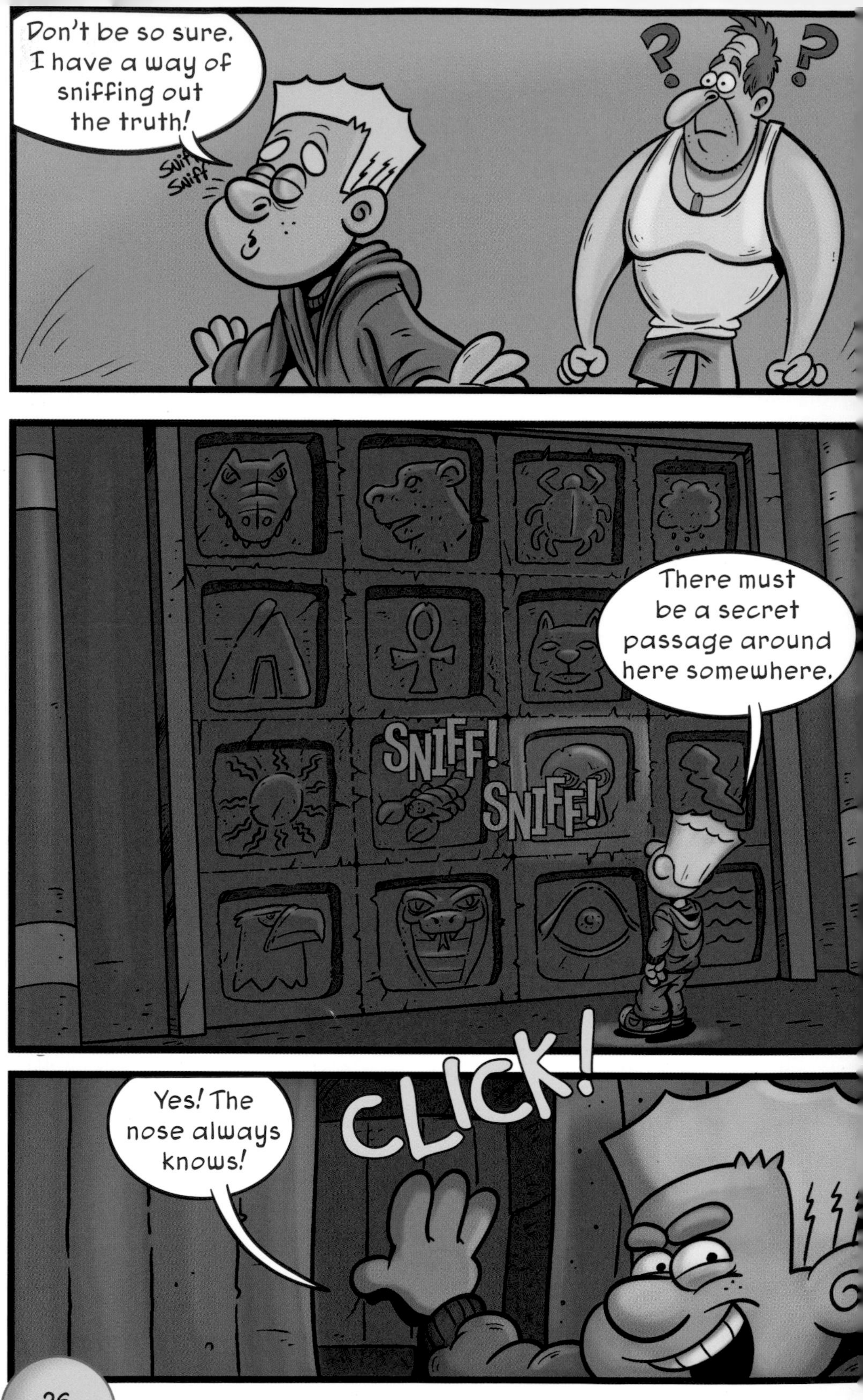
Don't be so sure. I have a way of sniffing out the truth!
Sniff Sniff
There must be a secret passage around here somewhere.
SNIFF!
SNIFF!
CLICK!
Yes! The nose always knows!

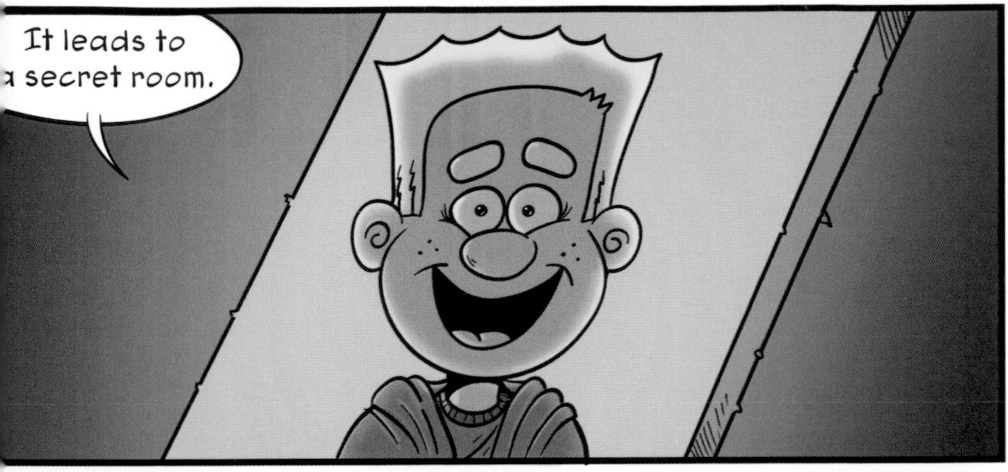

It leads to a secret room.

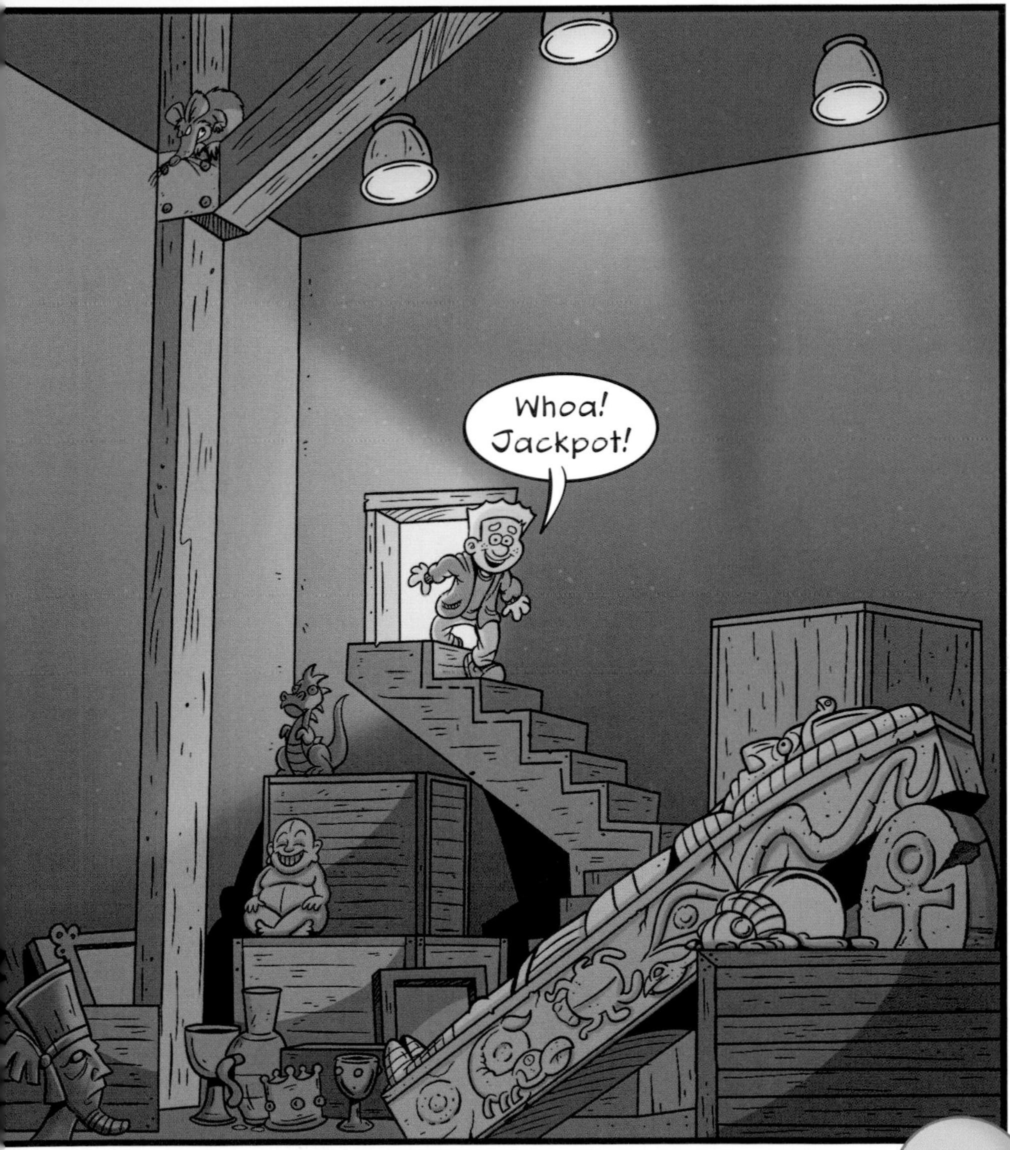

Whoa! Jackpot!

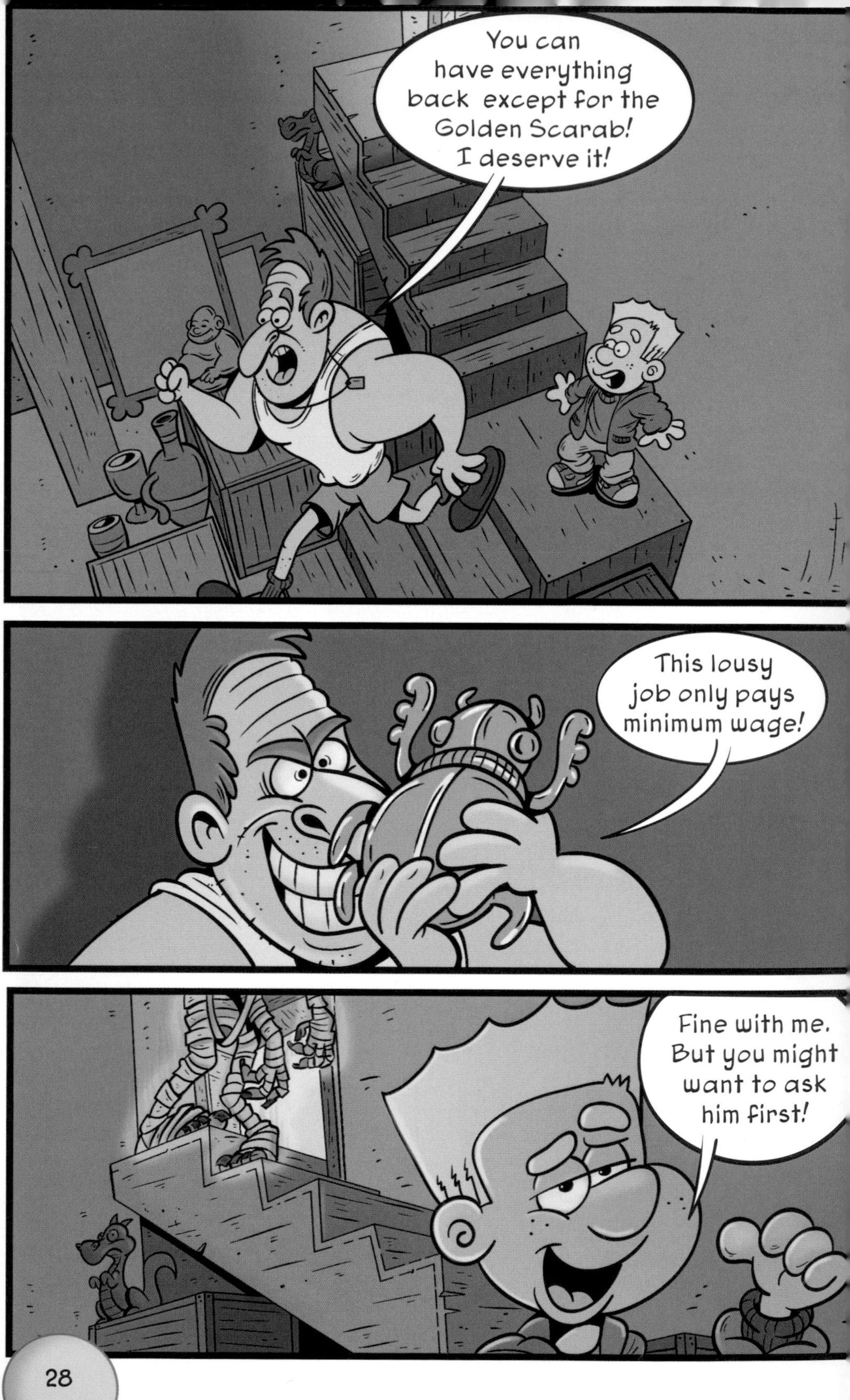
You can have everything back except for the Golden Scarab! I deserve it!
This lousy job only pays minimum wage!
Fine with me. But you might want to ask him first!

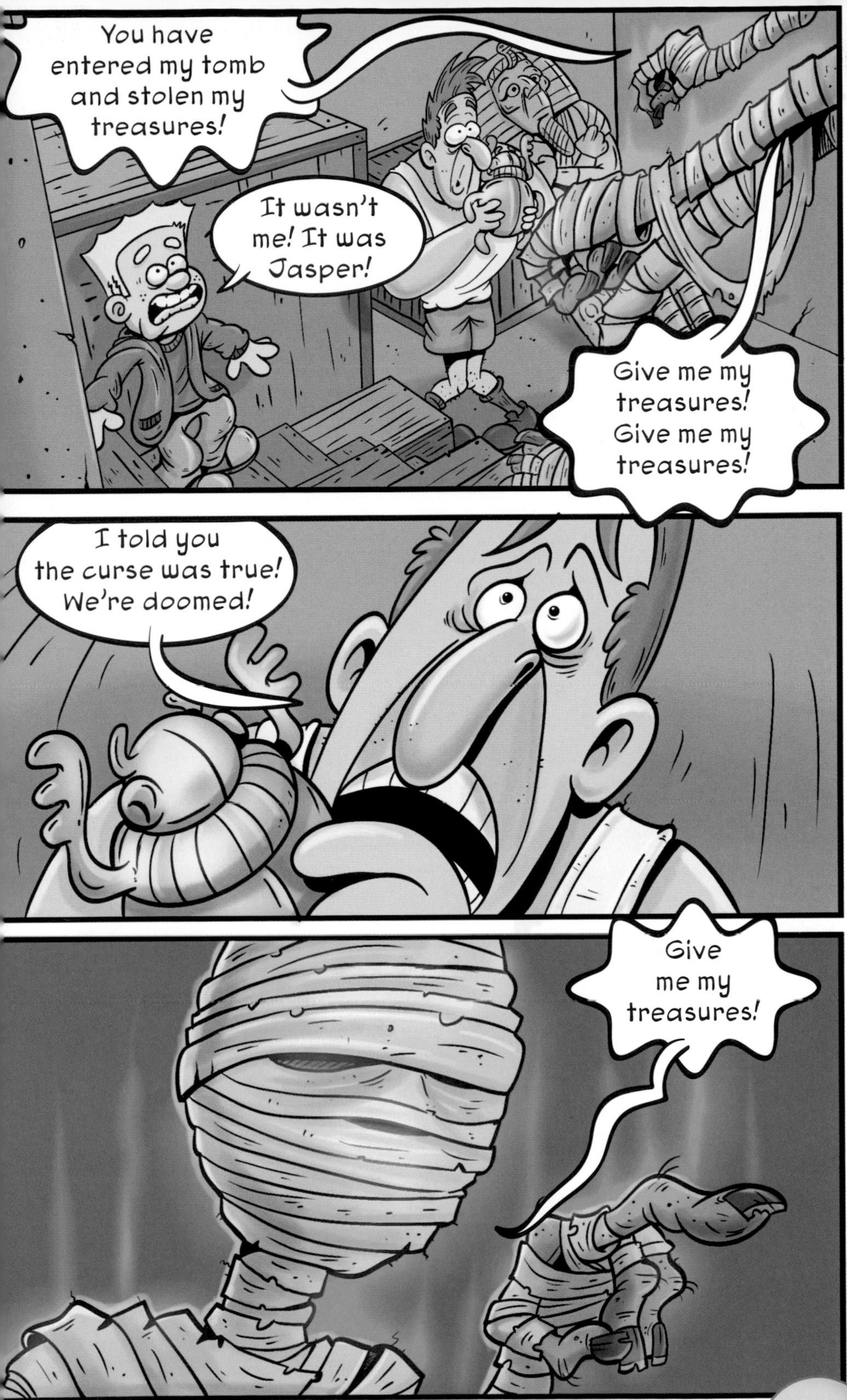
You have entered my tomb and stolen my treasures!
It wasn't me! It was Jasper!
Give me my treasures! Give me my treasures!
I told you the curse was true! We're doomed!
Give me my treasures!

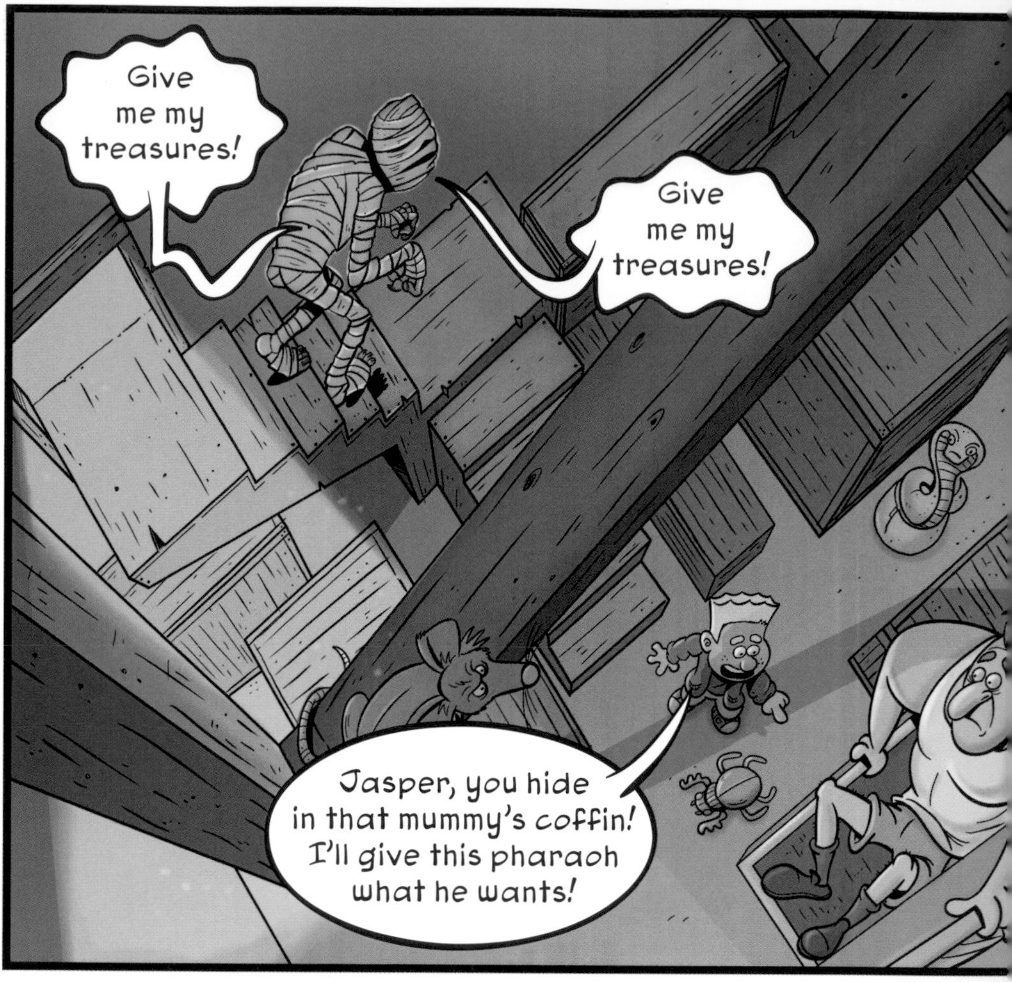
Give me my treasures!
Give me my treasures!
Jasper, you hide in that mummy's coffin! I'll give this pharaoh what he wants!

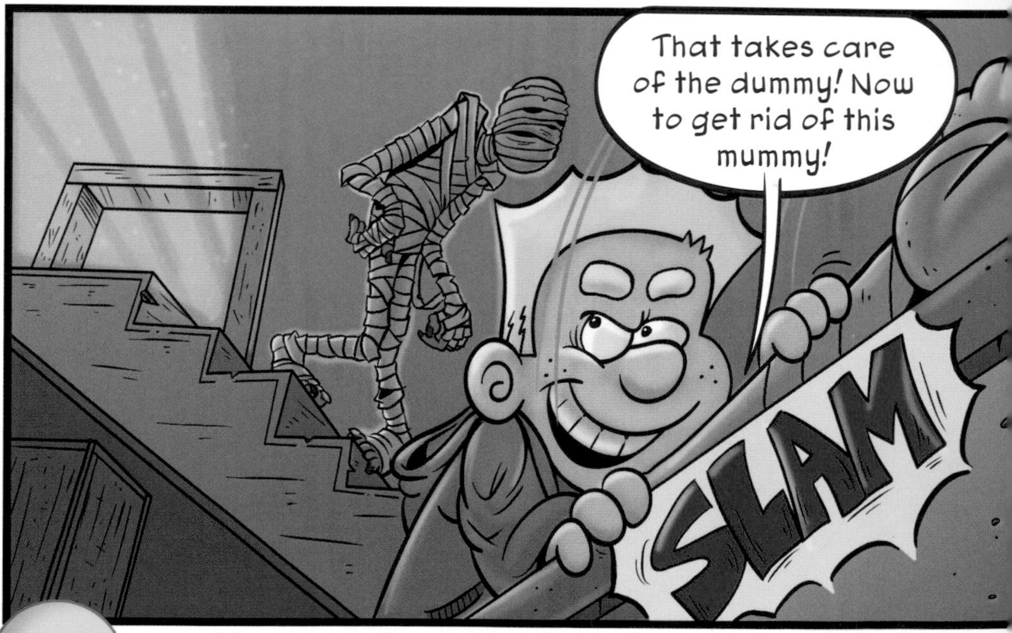
That takes care of the dummy! Now to get rid of this mummy!
SLAM

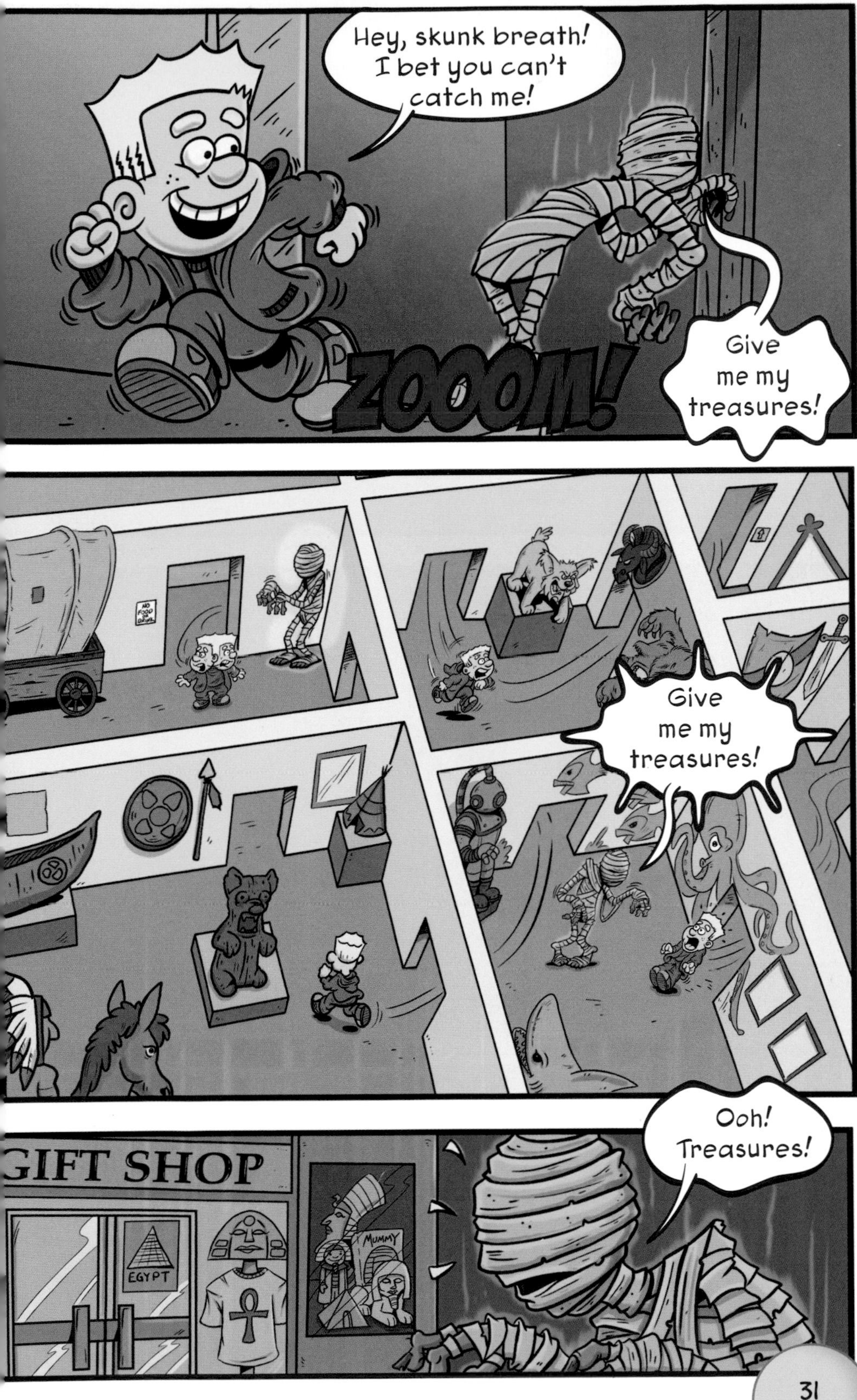
Hey, skunk breath! I bet you can't catch me!
ZOOOM!
Give me my treasures!
NO FOOD OR DRINK
Give me my treasures!
GIFT SHOP
EGYPT
MUMMY
Ooh! Treasures!

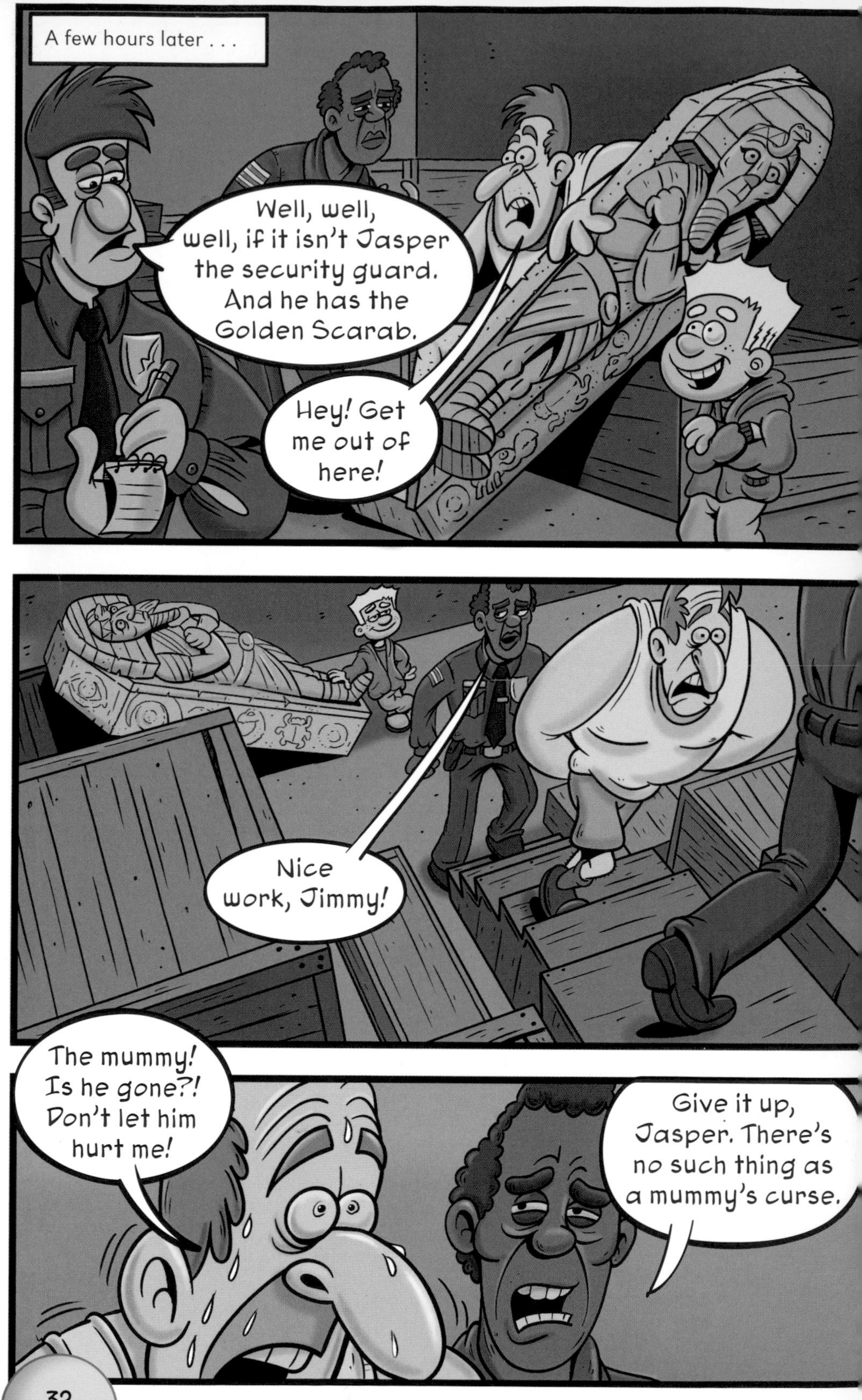
A few hours later . . .
Well, well, well, if it isn't Jasper the security guard. And he has the Golden Scarab.
Hey! Get me out of here!
Nice work, Jimmy!
The mummy! Is he gone?! Don't let him hurt me!
Give it up, Jasper. There's no such thing as a mummy's curse.

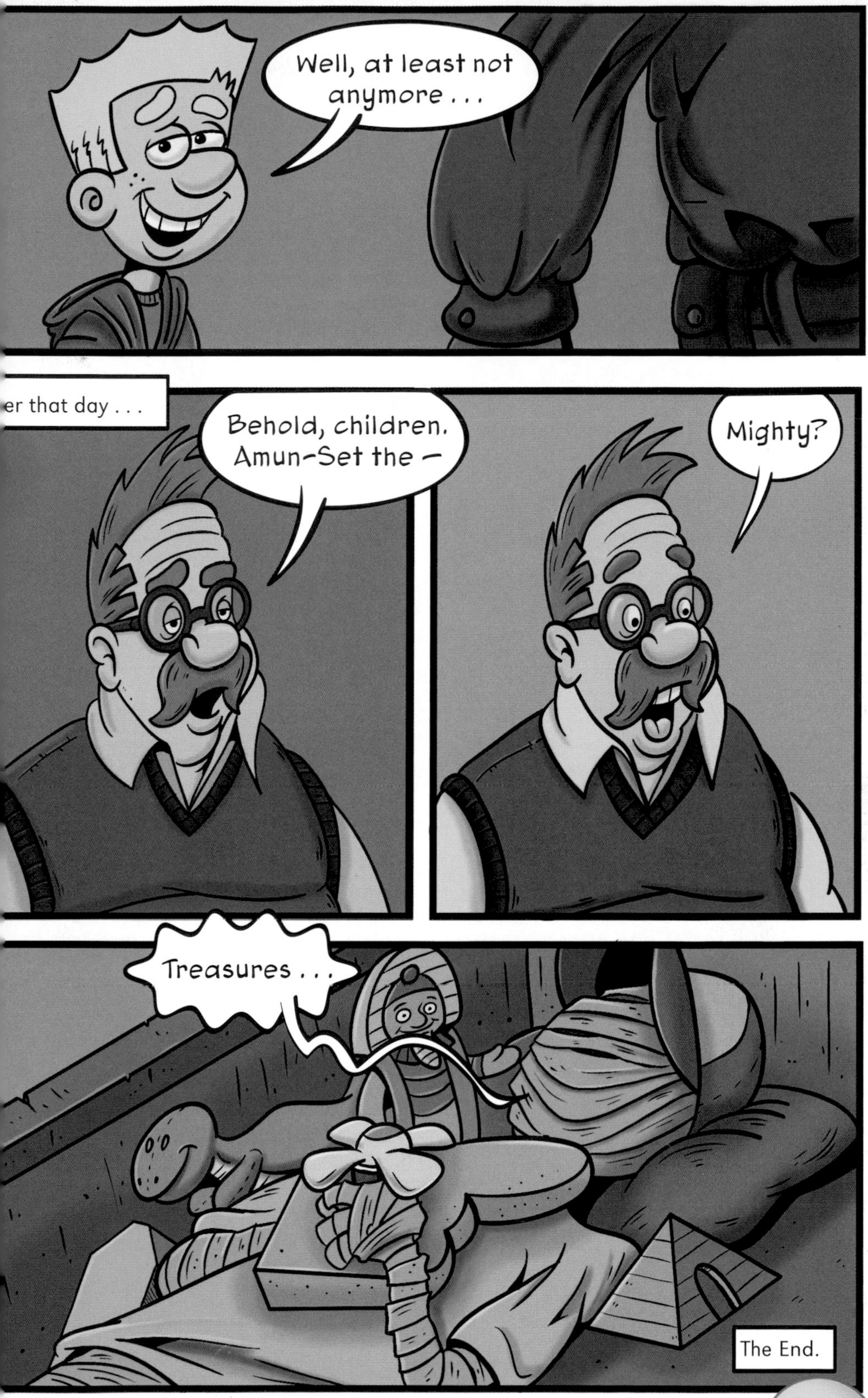
Well, at least not anymore . . .
er that day . . .
Behold, children. Amun-Set the —
Mighty?
Treasures . . .
The End.

ABOUT THE AUTHOR

Born in 1962 in Denver, Colorado, Scott Nickel works by day at Paws, Inc., Jim Davis's famous Garfield studio, and he freelances by night. Burning the midnight oil, Scott has created hundreds of humorous greeting cards and written several children's books, short fiction for *Boys' Life* magazine, comic strips, and lots of really funny knock-knock jokes. He was raised in southern California, but in 1995 Scott moved to Indiana, where he currently lives with his wife, two sons, six cats, and several sea monkeys.

ABOUT THE ILLUSTRATOR

Steve Harpster has loved drawing funny cartoons, mean monsters, and goofy gadgets since he was able to pick up a pencil. In first grade, he avoided writing assignments by working on the pictures for stories instead. Steve was able to land a job drawing funny pictures for books, and that's really what he's best at. Steve lives in Columbus, Ohio, with his wonderful wife, Karen, and their sheepdog, Doodle.

GLOSSARY

aftershave (AF-tur-shayv)—a scented lotion applied to the face after shaving

artifacts (ART-uh-fakts)—ancient objects made or used by humans

coffin (KAWF-in)—a long wooden container that holds a dead body

decay (di-KAY)—to decline in quality or break down

extinct (ek-STINGKT)—died out or no longer exists

legend (LEJ-uhnd)—a story handed down from long ago

minimum wage (MIN-uh-muhm WAJE)—the lowest amount of money a worker can be paid

pharaoh (FAIR-oh)—a ruler of ancient Egypt

scarab (SKAIR-uhb)—an ancient beetle that was very important to the ancient Egyptians

tomb (TOOM)—a grave, room, or building used for storing a dead body

MORE ABOUT MUMMIES

The most well known mummy in the world is King Tut or Tutankhamen. He was just 10 years old when he became the pharaoh of Egypt more than 3,000 years ago. He was mummified when he died as a teenager.

In the early 1920s, Lord Carnarvon and archaeologist Howard Carter of England found King Tut's tomb. They entered King Tut's burial chambers on February 17, 1923, in Egypt's Valley of the Kings. Weeks later, Lord Carnarvon died from a mosquito bite and pneumonia. The media reported the event, causing many people to believe that King Tut's tomb was cursed.

In ancient Egypt, almost all wealthy people were preserved as mummies after they died. They were buried with their riches, food, treasures, and sometimes servants and animals.

A mummy's major internal organs were removed and placed in jars. The only organ not removed was the heart.

In medieval times, buying and selling mummies was a profitable business. For that reason, grave robberies were quite common. People wanted the mummies and treasures to sell.

In the Victorian Era, unwrapping mummies was a popular hobby. Someone would buy a mummy and host a party. Unwrapping the mummy was the night's entertainment.

DISCUSSION QUESTIONS

1. Jimmy lies to his mom so he can go back to the museum after school. Was lying to his mom a good idea? Explain your answer.

2. Jimmy hides in the museum to catch the criminal. If you had to hide in a museum, where would you hide, and why?

3. Jasper tried to steal a lot of different artifacts from the museum. If you were the police, how would you punish him?

Cool!

WRITING PROMPTS

1. Jimmy and his class see lots of different treasures at the museum. Write a story about the type of museum you would like to visit.

2. What would happen to Jimmy Sniffles's nose powers if he caught a cold? Do you think he could still do his job? Write about it.

3. At the end of the story, the pharaoh comes alive and goes after his treasures. Create another ghost or mummy to help the pharaoh get his treasures back. Make sure to give him or her a name.

INTERNET SITES

The book may be over, but the adventure is just beginning.

Do you want to read more about the subjects or ideas in this book? Want to play cool games or watch videos about the authors who write these books? Then go to FactHound. At *www.facthound.com*, you'll be able to do all that, and more. The FactHound website can also send you to other safe Internet sites.

Check it out!